"You do not have to carry me upstairs."

Looking into Nicole's green eyes, Slade narrowed his gaze. "Because you don't want this?"

"Oh, I want whatever this is, but you don't have to lug me up the staircase to get it."

He chuckled. Yep, like no other high-maintenance society girl he'd ever met.

"No lugging required. You're as light as a feather."

"That may be, but I just survived a sniper's bullet and an attack on the train. I'm not going to risk tumbling down the stairs, even if I do end up on top of a hot navy SEAL."

"You don't have to take a fall down the stairs to wind up on top of this navy SEAL."

ALPHA BRAVO SEAL

CAROL ERICSON

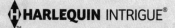

To Joanne, my trusty treasurer

Recycling programs
for this product may
not exist in your area.

ISBN-13: 978-1-335-72098-6

Alpha Bravo SEAL

Copyright © 2017 by Carol Ericson

Printed in U.S.A.

www.Harlequin.com

Carol Ericson is a bestselling, award-winning author of more than forty books. She has an eerie fascination for true-crime stories, a love of film noir and a weakness for reality TV, all of which fuel her imagination to create her own tales of murder, mayhem and mystery. To find out more about Carol and her current projects, please visit her website at www.carolericson.com, "where romance flirts with danger."

Books by Carol Ericson

Harlequin Intrigue

Red, White and Built

Locked, Loaded and SEALed
Alpha Bravo SEAL

Target: Timberline

Single Father Sheriff
Sudden Second Chance
Army Ranger Redemption
In the Arms of the Enemy

Brothers in Arms: Retribution

Under Fire
The Pregnancy Plot
Navy SEAL Spy
Secret Agent Santa

Harlequin Intrigue Noir

Toxic

Visit the Author Profile page at Harlequin.com for more titles.

CAST OF CHARACTERS

Nicole Hastings—A documentary filmmaker who lives life on the edge, she finally pushes the envelope too far and must join forces with the navy SEAL sniper who already rescued her once, but this time the danger fuels an attraction that might burn them both.

Slade Gallagher—This navy SEAL sniper rescued Nicole from Somali pirates but now must protect her from an evil in her own backyard, and this time saving Nicole is a lot more up close and personal than seeing her through the scope of his sniper rifle.

Lars Rasmussen—Nicole's cameraman has captured some footage that everyone wants to see, but anyone who possesses the film will get a target on his back.

Dave Pullman—He might be Lars's friend, but Dave is not willing to die for that friendship.

Giles Wentworth—A member of Nicole's film crew who died in a tragic car accident, or did he?

Trudy Waxman—Her friendship with Lars leads this actress to play a role that could mean life or death.

Conrad Walz—Trudy's boyfriend might be jealous of her friendship with Lars, or he might be an impostor.

Dahir Musse—Nicole's translator and guide in Somalia has gone missing since their kidnapping by pirates, but when he resurfaces he has a secret for Nicole that she may not want to hear.

Vlad—A sniper for the insurgents during the Gulf War caused trouble for Slade's sniper team, but a wartime clash has turned into a personal vendetta.

Ariel—The mysterious person on the other end of an email address giving orders to Slade on his mission.

Prologue

Slade Gallagher sucked in a salty breath of air and got ready for the kill.

Oblivious to the sniper rifles pointed at their heads from the yacht bobbing on the water just over three hundred feet away from them, four Somali pirates held their hostages at gunpoint as they communicated their demands to the two men who'd boarded their rickety craft. The two were US Navy seamen, but the pirates didn't know that—didn't need to.

The relatively calm seas made tracking his target easy—and safe for the hostage.

Slade zeroed in on his target, his dark skin glistening in the sun, one skinny arm wrapped around the hostage's throat, gun nestled beneath her ear. Slade's focus shifted to the hostage, a young woman with light brown hair blowing across her face and a tall, thin body, taut and ready.

What the hell was a woman doing out here in the Gulf of Aden? The orders for this assignment had made clear that this rescue didn't involve a cargo ship. This time the Somali pirates had captured a documentary film crew. *Idiots.*

Not that Slade couldn't understand the thrill of risk taking, but he preferred risks that pitted him against a big wave or a cave on the ocean floor, not desperate men in desperate situations.

The negotiator waved his arm once and shifted his body to the right, giving the SEAL snipers their first signal and a clear view of all four pirates. Slade licked the salt from his lips and coiled his muscles. He adjusted the aim on his M107.

The snipers had to drop their targets at the same time—or risk the lives of the hostages. He tracked back to the pretty brunette, now scooping her hair into a ponytail with one hand and tilting her head away from her captor. *Good girl.*

Had the negotiators been able to hint to the hostages that a team of Navy SEAL snipers was on the boat drifting off their starboard and watching their every move? It didn't matter. The men on deck would make their best assessment and the snipers would take action.

It wouldn't be pretty. That tall drink of water would suffer some blood spatter—but at least it wouldn't be her own. He'd make sure of that.

The other negotiator held both hands out in supplication, the final signal, and Slade set his timer to five seconds. He murmured along for the count. "Five, four, three, two…"

He took the shot. All four pirates jerked at once in a macabre dance and fell to the deck.

Slade inched his scope to the woman he'd just saved. She hadn't fainted dead away, screamed or jumped up and down. She formed an X over her chest with her blood-spattered arms, looked down at the dead pirate and spit on his body.

Hauling back his sniper rifle, Slade shook his head.

That was one crazy chick—just his type.

Chapter One

Eighteen months later

A sick feeling rose in Nicole's gut as she skimmed the online article. The rumor was true. She hunched forward, reading aloud. "'Freelance cameraman Lars Rasmussen was found dead of an apparent suicide in his parents' home in the Hellerup district of Copenhagen.'"

She stopped reading and slumped in her chair. "No way."

Lars, with his sunny smile and scruffy goatee, wasn't even acquainted with the word *depression*.

Nicole grabbed her cell phone and scrolled through her contacts. Lars had picked his brother, Ove, as his emergency contact, and she'd kept all of those numbers. Maybe she'd had a premonition.

She squinted at the time on her computer screen, hoping Ove was an early riser. She tapped his number, which already contained the international calling code for Denmark, and placed the call.

He picked up after two rings. *"Hej."*

"Hello. Is this Ove Rasmussen?"

"Yes. Who's this, please?" He'd switched to English seamlessly.

"This is Nicole Hastings. I worked with your brother, Lars, on a couple of projects."

"Of course, Nicole. My brother mentioned you often."

"I heard the news about his death, and I just wanted to tell you how sorry I am." *And to give you the third degree.*

"Yes, yes. Thank you. It was a shock."

"Was he? I mean, what…?" She closed her eyes and shoved a hand through her tangled hair. "What I mean to say is, I can't believe Lars would take his own life."

Ove drew in a sharp breath. "Yes, well, some girl trouble, a failed project."

Ove didn't know his brother very well if he thought a woman could send Lars over the edge, but she couldn't argue with a bereaved family member.

She loosened her death grip on the phone. "I'm so sorry. He was a good guy and a helluva cameraman."

"That's how I know he must've been depressed."

"How?" Her pulse ticked up a notch.

"When we…discovered his body, we couldn't find any of his cameras in the house. He'd been staying with our parents after his last project, the one after the debacle in Somalia. He had been working on a local story about the Syrian refugees in Denmark."

"His cameras? Why would he get rid of his cameras?"

Ove sighed across the miles. "I don't know, Nicole. He mentioned you, though, a few weeks before he died. You were with him when you all got kidnapped in Somalia, right?"

"Yes." Her pounding heart rattled her rib cage. "What did he say?"

"Just that he was sorry the film never got released, because he'd captured some amazing footage. He was thinking about contacting you about the project, reviving it, turning the film over to you."

"He never did." She tapped one fingernail on the edge of her laptop. "Did he happen to mention Giles Wentworth, too? He was another member of our film crew."

"Giles. English guy, right?"

"That's right." Nicole held her breath.

"Not lately. I don't think so. I don't remember."

"I was just wondering because… Giles passed away a few months ago."

Ove spewed out a Danish word that sounded like an expletive. "Not suicide?"

"A car accident in Scotland."

"That's a shame. It would seem that story you were trying to capture in Somalia was bad luck."

"It would seem so." She bit her lip, toying with the

phrasing of her next question. "D-did Lars—was he worried about anything before his death?"

"Just that woman." He released a noisy breath. "I have to go to work now, Nicole. Thank you for calling."

"Of course. My condolences again on your loss."

"And, Nicole?"

"Yes?"

"It sounds like you need to be careful."

When she ended the call, she folded her arms over her stomach, gripping her elbows. Ove had been referring to the coincidence of two of the film crew dying within months of each other, but Nicole wasn't so sure it was a coincidence.

She pushed back from the desk and sauntered to the window overlooking the street below. Even at 2:00 a.m., taxis zipped to and fro, and the occasional pedestrian ambled along the sidewalk, two blocks up from Central Park.

Nicole caught her breath when she spied a figure under the green awning of the brownstone across the street, his pale face tilted toward her window. Twitching the drape, she stepped back and peered from the edge of its heavy folds.

She'd dimmed the lights in the apartment earlier, only the glow of her computer screen illuminating her workspace. Someone ten floors down wouldn't be able to see her at the window.

Then why was her heart racing and her palms

sweating? This was the first time she'd noticed a suspicious person outside her building, but not the first time in the past few months she'd felt watched, followed, spied upon.

Her fear had started, not just with news of Giles's accident, but with his death along with her inability to reach Dahir, the Somali translator who'd been a part of their film crew. She still hadn't located Dahir, and rumors swirling around Lars had sent her into a panic. Now that she'd confirmed Lars's passing, a strange calm had settled about her shoulders like a heavy cape.

Four people on that film crew, four people held hostage by Somali pirates, four people rescued by the Navy SEALs, two of those people dead eighteen months later, one missing and…her. Was this just some bizarre twist of fate, claiming the lives of people who should've died a year and a half ago? That sort of stuff only happened in horror movies.

The man across the street made a move, and she peered into the darkness as he emerged from beneath the awning and loped down the sidewalk. Her eyes followed him until the night swallowed him whole at the end of the block.

She huffed out a breath and drew the drapes. She'd planned an extended stay in New York while her mother hit Europe for the fashion shows—starting with Paris in March and winding up with Rome in July. Maybe she should get a bodyguard.

Nicole turned and surveyed the office of the lavishly furnished Upper East Side apartment where her mother had lived for years. It wasn't like she couldn't afford a 24/7 bodyguard.

A bodyguard for what? Who could possibly have it in for a documentary film crew that hadn't even managed to release the movie about the underground feminist movement in Somalia? The women they'd met had reason to fear for their lives, but after the kidnapping their translator had gone into hiding and the rest of them had scattered, abandoning the project.

Nicole hadn't even seen the footage Lars had shot—and it must've been good if he'd mentioned it to his brother. As talented as he was, Lars wasn't one to puff out his chest.

She planted herself in front of her computer again, and her fingers flew across the keyboard in a desperate search for Dahir Musse. She'd lobbied to get Dahir out of Somalia after the kidnapping incident, but even her mother's political connections hadn't been able to get the job done.

If they had, would Dahir be alive today instead of missing in action? Or would he be just as dead as Giles and Lars? Just as dead as she might be?

THE NEXT MORNING, heavy eyed and yawning, Nicole sucked down the rest of her smoothie and tossed the cup in the trash can on her way back to the counter.

Skye raised her eyebrows. "Ready for another?"

"Just a shot of wheatgrass. If I hope to get in even two miles today, I need a little energy."

"You look tired. Late night at the clubs?"

"I wish." She swept up the little paper cup Skye had placed before her and downed the foul-tasting liquid in one gulp. Then she crushed the cup in her hand. "See ya."

Skye waved as Nicole pushed out the door of the shop. Leaning forward, she braced her foot on the side of the building to tie the loose laces of her running shoe. She caught a movement out of the corner of her eye—a man walking on the sidewalk across the street.

She bent over farther but slid her gaze sideways to watch the tall, lean guy lope down the block—*lope*. He had a distinctive rangy, loose-limbed gait, one she'd seen in the wee hours of the morning across the street from her building.

Narrowing her eyes, she watched his back, the sun gleaming off his blond hair. Now that she'd confirmed Lars's death, her paranoia was going into overdrive. The man hadn't looked at her once, and he certainly wasn't following her.

She straightened up and rolled back her shoulders. She needed that run more than ever, and the fresh greenery of the park beckoned. She launched forward with one last glance over her shoulder, then tripped to a stop.

He wasn't following her because he was heading for her apartment. To lie in wait? To break in?

She abandoned her run and made a U-turn in the street. She didn't want to confront the man, but two could play the stalking game. Veering to the left, she cut in one street ahead of her own. If she came into the building's lobby through the back way, she might catch him trying to get through the front door. Leo, the doorman, might have something to say about that.

Nicole tightened her ponytail and turned down the alley that led to the back of her building. She might be way off here, but something about that man had seemed familiar. If he wasn't hanging around trying to get into the building, she'd go for her run with a clear mind—at least as clear as it could be while worrying about the mysterious deaths of her colleagues.

When she got to the apartment, she pulled her key ring from the little pocket in the back of her running shirt and plucked out the building key.

She slid it into the lock and eased open the door. Flattening herself against the wall, she sidled along toward the mailboxes. If she peered around the corner of the hallway where the mailboxes stretched out in three rows, she'd have a clear view of the lobby and the front door.

She crept around the corner and jerked back, dropping her keys with a clatter.

The tall stranger, his gleaming hair covered with

the hood of his sweatshirt, glanced up, the mail from her box clutched in his hands.

She should've turned and run away, but a whip of fury lashed her body and she lunged forward.

"What the hell are you doing going through my mail?"

Then her stalker did the most amazing thing.

A smile broke across his tanned face, and he lifted a pair of broad shoulders. "Guess you caught me red-handed, Nicole."

Chapter Two

The color drained from her face as fast as it had flared red in her cheeks. "Do I know you? And even if I do, I'm about two seconds from screaming bloody murder for the doorman and getting the cops out here."

He believed her. A woman who would risk sailing the dangerous Gulf of Aden just to get a story wouldn't fear some creeper in New York City—not that he was a creeper.

"Sorry about the mail." He fanned out some bills and a few ads. "I'm not very good at this."

"Good at what?" She inched past him and the row of mailboxes until she had one foot in the lobby.

"Skulking, I guess."

"Are you going to tell me what you're doing, or am I going to call the NYPD?" She jabbed her cell phone into the space between them.

"You see? I suck at this." He bundled her mail, which he hadn't had a chance to look at, and held it out to her. "I'm Slade Gallagher, the US Navy SEAL sniper who saved your life eighteen months ago off the coast of Somalia."

She blinked, licked her lips and edged closer to him. "Is this some kind of trick?"

Trick? What kind of trick would that be? He stuffed his free hand into the pocket of his sweatshirt and withdrew his wallet. He flipped it open with one hand, his other still gripping the mail she'd refused to take from him.

"Take it and look at the card behind my driver's license. It's my military ID. Hell, look at my driver's license, too."

She reached forward to take the wallet from him between two fingers, as if stealing something from a snake ready to strike.

"And if my ID isn't good enough for you, I can tell you what you were wearing that day." He closed his eyes as if picturing the scene all over again through his scope. "You had on army-green cargo pants, a loose red shirt and a khaki jacket, with a red scarf wrapped around your neck."

His lids flew open, and Nicole was staring at him through wide green eyes. She might be surprised, but he'd pictured the woman on the boat—Nicole Hastings—many times over the past year and a half. Some nights he couldn't get the picture of her out of his head.

"We never knew your names. The Navy wouldn't

tell us." She traced a finger over his driver's license picture behind the plastic, and his face tingled as if she'd brushed it. "But while we were in the infirmary getting checked out, we saw you walking toward the helicopter before you boarded it and left the boat. I do recognize you."

Her sculpted eyebrows collided over her nose. "But what are you doing here? Why have you been following me?"

"Following you?" A pulse hummed in his throat. "I just got here two days ago."

"Last night?"

"I was watching your building." He shook his head. "Damn, you noticed me out there?"

"Yes. Why are you watching me?"

"I hadn't planned on having this discussion with you so early, but it works out better for me if we do." He jerked his thumb at the ceiling. "Can we continue this conversation in your apartment?"

Her gaze shifted toward the lobby and back to his face.

"You can introduce me to the doorman and tell him we're going up to your place. In fact, that's the smart thing to do."

She snapped his wallet closed and thrust it at him, and then spun on her heel. He followed her, still clutching the mail.

The doorman leaped into action and swung the

door open for her before she reached it. "I didn't see you come in, Nicole."

"Came in through the back door." She leveled a finger at Slade. "This is a…my friend. He's coming up to my place, Leo, in case you see him wandering around the building."

Leo tilted his head. "Okay. Nice to meet you. Any friend of the Hastings women has gotta be good people."

Slade swept the hood from his head and held out his free hand. "Slade Gallagher."

"Leo Veneto."

Slade glanced at the tattoo on Leo's forearm. "Marine?"

"Yes, sir. Tenth Marine regiment, artillery force. Served in the first Gulf War."

Slade pumped his hand. "Hoorah."

"Hoorah." Leo gave Slade the once-over. "Navy, right?"

"You got it—SEAL sniper."

"You boys saved our asses more than a few times."

Nicole broke up the handshake and the mutual admiration. "We're going to go up now."

Leo grinned. "I'll be right here."

Slade followed her to the elevator where she stabbed the call button and turned to him suddenly. "I never knew Leo was in the Marines."

"Has *Semper Fi* tattooed right on his arm."

She finally snatched the mail from his hands as

the doors of the elevator whisked open. "See anything interesting in my mail?"

"You didn't give me a chance to go through all of it, but it looks like Harvard's hitting you up for a donation."

"They wouldn't dare. I'm not even an alumna, and my father already funded a library for them."

"So why'd you go to NYU instead of Harvard, where I'm sure they would've found a spot for you?"

"Film school." She narrowed her eyes. "It's not all family connections, you know."

"Doesn't hurt." He should know.

They rode up to the tenth floor in silence, but he could practically hear all the gears shifting in her head, forming questions. He didn't blame her. He just didn't know if he'd have any answers that would satisfy her—rather than scare the spit out of her.

The elevator jolted to a stop on the tenth floor, and he held the door as she stepped out. "No penthouse suite, huh?"

"My mom didn't want to be too ostentatious." Her lips twisted. "And I'm being serious."

Still, there seemed to be just two apartments on this floor. The size and location of this place must've run her mother, Mimi Hastings, more than five mil.

Nicole swung open the door with a flourish and watched him out of the corner of her eye as she stepped aside.

His gaze swept from one side of the opulently

furnished room to the other, taking in the gold brocade sofas, the marble tables, the blindingly white
carpet, the curved staircase to another floor and the
artwork he could guarantee was worth a fortune.
"Impressive."

"This is my mother's place. I'm here watching
the…"

Before she could finish the sentence, a ball of
white fur shot out from somewhere in the back of
the apartment and did a couple of somersaults before
landing at Slade's feet, paws scrabbling for purchase
against the legs of his jeans.

She rolled her eyes. "That's a dog, believe it or
not, and I'm taking care of her for my mother."

Slade crouched and tickled the excited Shih Tzu
beneath the chin. "Hey, little guy."

"It's a girl, and her name is Chanel."

"Let me guess." He straightened up. "She has a
diamond collar."

"You pretty much have my mom all figured out."

"Where is she, your mother?"

"Are we discussing my mother or why a Navy
SEAL is spying on me in Manhattan?" She crossed
her arms and tapped the toe of her running shoe.

He waved his arm at a deep-cushioned chair. "Can
I sit down first? Maybe something to drink? This
spying is tough business."

Her lips formed a thin line, and for a minute he
thought she was going to refuse. "All right."

"Water is fine, and I'll even get it myself if you show me the way."

She crooked her finger. "Follow me, but no more stalling."

Was that what he was doing? He had to admit, he didn't want to be the bearer of bad news—and he had bad news for Nicole Hastings.

The little dog jumped into the chair he was eyeing, so he followed Nicole's swaying hips, the Lycra of her leggings hugging every gentle line of her body. She was thin, but curved in and out in all the right places.

As she passed a granite island in the center of the kitchen, she kicked the leg of a stool tucked beneath the counter. "Have a seat."

She yanked open the door of the fridge. "I have water, sparkling water, iced tea, juice, soda, beer and a 2008 Didier Dagueneau sauvignon blanc—a very good year."

Was she trying to show off, or did that stuff just roll from her lips naturally? "Sparkling water, please."

She filled two glasses with ice and then set them down in the middle of the island. The bottle with a green and yellow label hissed as she twisted off its lid, and the liquid fizzed and bubbled when it hit the ice.

She shoved a glass toward him. "Now that the formalities are over, let's get to the main event."

"You don't mess around, do you?"

"I didn't think you'd be one to mess around, either, the way you dropped that pirate who had me at gunpoint."

"This is different." He took a sip of the water, the bubbles tickling his nose. "You know that Giles Wentworth died in a car accident last February?"

"Went off the road in Scotland."

"A few weeks ago, Lars Rasmussen committed suicide—took an overdose of pills."

"I know that." She hunched over the counter, drilling him with her green eyes. "What I want to know is the location and general health of Dahir Musse."

He took a bigger gulp of his drink than he'd intended, and it fizzed in his nose. He wiped his eyes with the heel of his hand. "You've already connected the dots."

"I don't know if I've connected any dots, but Giles has driven on some incredibly dangerous roads without getting one scratch on the car, and Lars was about the least depressed person I know. Girl trouble?" She snorted, her delicate nostrils flaring. "He had a woman in every port, literally."

Had she been one of those women?

The thought had come out of left field, and Slade took a careful sip of his water. "So, you already have a suspicion the deaths of your friends weren't coincidental."

"It's not just that." She caught a drip of condensation on the outside of her glass with the tip of her finger and dragged it back to the rim. "You said you've been here in New York just a few days?"

"Yeah."

"I've had a feeling of being watched and followed for about two weeks now, ever since I heard rumors about Lars."

"Anything concrete?"

"Until I caught you going through my mailbox? No."

Heat crawled up his face to the roots of his hair. He'd tried to tell the brass he'd be no good at spying.

"You still haven't told me what you're doing here and why you were going through my mail."

"Someone who monitors these things—our rescues, I mean—noticed the deaths. This guy raised a red flag because there was a hit stateside on another person our team had rescued—a doctor who'd helped us out in Pakistan. That proved to be related to terrorist activity in the region."

She'd folded her hands around the glass, her white knuckles the only sign of tension. "You're telling me that someone is after the four of us? Do you know where Dahir Musse is?"

"We don't know where he is, and I can't tell you for sure that someone is out to get your film crew, but I'm here to find out."

"A Navy SEAL operating in the US? Isn't that illegal or something?"

"Not exactly, but it is top secret. I'm not really here." He pressed a finger to his lips. "I am sorry about the loss of your friends."

"Thanks." Her chest rose and fell as the corner of her mouth twitched. "Giles's mother called to tell me about the accident. At the time, I figured it was just that—an accident. Then a few weeks ago, I started hearing rumors that Lars had killed himself. That's about the time I started feeling watched. I put it down to paranoia at first, but the feelings got stronger. Then I verified Lars's death last night with his brother and seriously freaked out, especially since I saw you lurking across the street at two in the morning."

"Sorry about that. What were you doing up at two o'clock?"

"Working."

"Did you ever release that documentary? I looked for it but never saw anything about the movie."

Her eyes widened. "We never finished the film. We were all shaken up after the kidnapping and moved on to other projects—with other people."

"The film was about Somali women, right?"

"About Somali women and the underground feminist movement there—dangerous stuff."

He scratched the stubble on his chin. "That might be enough to get you killed."

"Maybe, but why now? We never finished the film, never discussed finishing it. I never even got my hands on the footage." She swirled her glass, and the ice tinkled against the side. "Are you here to figure out what's going on?"

"I'm here to…make sure it doesn't happen again."

"To me."

"To you."

"I have no idea why someone would be after us now. Why weren't we killed in Somalia if someone wanted to stop the film?"

"Our team of snipers stopped that from happening."

"Do you think that's why the pirates kidnapped us? I thought they were going for ransom. That's what they told us, anyway."

"The pirates patrolling those waters are usually working for someone else. They could've been hired to stop you and then once they were successful decided to go rogue and trade you for ransom money instead."

She waved her arms out to her sides. "We're in the middle of New York City. Do you know how crazy that sounds?"

"As crazy as it sounds in the middle of some Scottish highland road or in some posh district of Copenhagen."

"Do you have people looking for Dahir?"

"We do, but there's also the possibility that Dahir is working with the other side."

She landed a fist on the granite. "Never. I tried to

get him and his family out of Somalia. His life wasn't going to be worth much there after that rescue on the high seas. He'd become a target in Mogadishu even before Giles and Lars died."

"Tell me more about your feelings of being followed. Do you have any proof? Any evidence?" He watched her over the edge of his glass as he drained it.

Her instincts had been right about him following her, so she could be onto something. She might be a pampered rich girl, but she'd spent time in some of the most dangerous places in the world—and had survived.

"No hard evidence—a man on the subway who seemed to be following me, a persistent guy at a club one night, a jogger who kept turning up on the same trails in the park."

He studied her face with its high cheekbones, patrician nose and full lips and found it hard to believe she hadn't experienced persistent guys in clubs before. "These were all different men?"

"All different. I can't explain it. It's a general creep factor. I know you think because I come from a privileged background I don't have any street smarts, but I've been in some rough areas around the world. We do have to keep our wits about us or wind up in hot water."

"I believe you. I looked you up online." He wouldn't tell her that he'd researched Nicole Hastings long before he'd gotten this unusual assignment. She might start feeling a general creep factor about *him*.

"Who sent you here? The Navy?"

"I'm reporting directly to my superior officer in the Navy, but it goes beyond that. I'm also reporting to someone from the intelligence community— someone named Ariel."

"Why would the intelligence community be interested in a couple of documentary filmmakers getting into trouble with some Somali pirates?"

"I doubt a bunch of ragtag pirates have the reach and connections to commit two murders in Europe and make them look like accidents."

"So, the CIA or the FBI or whoever thinks our situation is linked to something or someone else?"

"Could be."

She tapped a manicured fingernail on his glass. "Do you want more water?"

"No, thanks."

As she tipped a bit more in her own glass, she said, "What did you hope to find in my mail, anyway?"

"I'm not sure. I'm a sniper, not a spook. I was just checking out what I could."

"And what did you discover other than a request from Harvard?" She moved out of the kitchen with the grace of a gazelle and swept the mail from a table where she'd dropped it.

Hunching forward on his stool, he said, "Nothing.

I wasn't lying when I told you I didn't have a chance to look through it all."

She returned, shuffling through the large stack of envelopes and mailers. "Bills, junk, junk, bills, postcard from my mom, who's the only one I know who still sends them instead of texting pictures. More bills…"

Her face paled as she plucked an envelope from the fanned-out pieces of mail.

"What is it?"

"It's a letter from Lars—from beyond the grave."

Chapter Three

Nicole held the thin envelope between two fingers, fear pulsing through every fiber of her being, her mouth suddenly dry.

Slade launched from his stool and hovered over her shoulder. "How do you know it's from Lars? There's no return address, and it definitely wasn't sent from Denmark."

"I'd recognize his chicken scratch anywhere." She flicked the postmark with her fingernail. "New York, not Denmark."

"Was he in the city?"

"Not that I know of, but then, I haven't even been here a month."

"Are you going to open it or stare at it for a while?"

He was practically breathing down her neck, so she took a few steps to her left. She ripped into the envelope, and a single sheet of white paper fluttered to the counter.

As Slade reached for it, she snatched it up and squinted at it. "His handwriting always was atrocious."

"Do you want me to try?"

"It says—" she plastered the note against the granite and ran her finger beneath the squiggle of words "—'I instructed my friend to mail this letter to you if anything happens to me.'"

She gasped and covered her mouth. "He knew."

"Go on." Slade rapped his knuckle on the counter next to the paper, clearly impatient for her to continue.

She wanted to read this in private, shed tears in her own way. But Slade was here to help. He'd saved her once, from a ramshackle boat in the Gulf of Aden, and she'd trust him in a heartbeat to do it again.

She took a deep breath and started reading. "'It's the film, Nic. Somebody wants that film we shot in Somalia. I gave it to my friend in New York and told him where to hide it, and I'm putting out the word that the footage was damaged during the hijacking of our boat. Maybe they'll leave me alone. Maybe they'll leave us alone. If nothing happens and you never get this note, I'll put it down to paranoia and we'll retrieve that footage and make a hell of a documentary. If I die, don't look for it, and watch your back. Whatever happens, it was great working with you, Nic.'"

A spasm of pain crumpled her face, and one hot tear dripped from her eye, hitting the back of her hand and rolling off to create a splotch on the paper. "Oh, my God. He must've known someone was after him, too."

"Who's this friend?" With his middle finger, Slade slid Lars's note toward his side of the counter. He studied the words on the page as if they could tell him more than what she'd just read.

"He didn't mention the friend's name." She flipped the envelope back over and ran her thumb across the postmark again. "It was mailed two days ago, so his friend must've waited to send it, unless he just learned of Lars's death."

"Do you know Lars's friends in New York?"

"I met a few of them, but just casually at a dinner once and then at a party in SoHo."

"Was the party given by one of his friends?"

"I think it was, but this was a few years ago. These were people I didn't know, so they must've been his friends."

"We need to find this guy." He smacked the note on the counter and drilled his knuckle into the middle of it.

"Maybe we shouldn't." She threaded her fingers in front of her and then couldn't stop twisting them. "Maybe I should keep spreading the story that the footage was damaged and unusable."

"Because that story worked so well for Lars?"

"If they hear it from both me and Lars and they

didn't find the film when they…killed Lars or Giles, maybe they'll believe it this time."

"If someone is looking for that footage, it must be important."

"Important?" She pressed the sweating glass against her cheek, hoping the cold moisture would bring her out of this nightmare. "It was footage of interviews with Somali women discussing education and property rights. I understand how that might mean something to the men in Mogadishu and the towns and villages where these women live, but I can't see those men traveling to Denmark or Scotland to carry out a hit to retrieve the footage."

"It must be something else, something one of the women said. Lars and Giles were murdered for a specific reason, not just because a few men were upset about the women's rights movement in Somalia."

She turned her back on Lars's note and put the bottled water back in the fridge. "I can't imagine what our interview subjects could've said that would get us in trouble—or how anyone would even know what they said."

"You conducted the interviews in private?"

"Of course we did. Those women were risking their lives talking to us."

"Who arranged the meetings?"

"Dahir. He was our translator as well as our facilitator. I tried to get him out." She rubbed the back of her hand across her tingling nose. "But the US government was uncooperative."

"The Navy has a hard time resettling people who help *us* out. I'm sure it's even more difficult for journalists to get their people out." He picked up the note and waved it at her. "We need to find out who sent this note for Lars and get him to turn over the film."

"I don't have any contact info for his friends here."

"What about that party? Do you remember where it was? Do you have any pictures? C'mon, people take pictures of their food. There must be something online. Social media sites?"

She snapped her fingers. "Lars was always filming at parties. It got pretty annoying, actually. He might've shared some video with me."

"That's a start."

"Follow me." She scooted past him out of the kitchen and crossed the living room to the small office she used when staying with Mom. Chanel woke up and trotted after them.

Leaning over the desk, Nicole shifted her mouse to wake up her computer and launched a social media site.

"How long ago was this party?" Slade crouched in front of the desk so the monitor was at his eye level.

"About two years ago, six months before we left for Somalia." She scrolled through the pictures on the left-hand side of her page, hoping Slade wasn't

paying attention to all the pics of her and her exes—
and she had a bunch. "Video, video."

"Wow, someone could follow your whole life on
here. You should be careful."

The hair on the back of her neck quivered. Anyone would know she ran in Central Park, hung out
with two of her best friends in Chelsea, visited a former professor at NYU. She'd opened up her life for
any stranger to track her. It hadn't seemed to matter...before.

Her heart skipped a beat. "Here! This is it."

As Slade scooted in closer to the monitor, Nicole
clicked on the video Lars had sent her of the party.
She turned up the volume on her computer, and party
sounds filtered from the speakers—voices, laughter,
music, clinking glasses.

Slade poked at the screen. "That's you. Giles is
behind you, right?"

She nodded and sniffled when she saw Giles's
wife wrap her arms around him from behind. "That's
his wife, Mila."

The camera shifted to three people crowded together on a love seat. "Do you know them? The man?
Lars referred to his friend with a masculine pronoun,
so we know it's a guy."

"He and the two women are Lars's friends. He's
not the owner of the loft, though. That would be…"
The camera swung wide, taking in two women and a

man dancing and giggling with drinks in their hands. "This guy. Paul something. He's Danish, also."

"Paul something, Danish guy who lives in a loft in SoHo. We can start there."

She ripped a piece of paper from a pad and grabbed a pen. "Paul, Dane, SoHo."

"Shh." He covered her writing hand with his. "Can you go back? Someone's shouting out names."

She clicked and dragged back the status bar on the video and released. In a singsong voice with slightly accented English, a man called out. "Go, Trudy, go, Teresa, go, Lundy."

Closing her eyes, Nicole said, "That's Lars."

"I'm assuming those are the dancers. Is his name Paul or Lundy? Or is Lundy his last name?"

Her lids flew open. "It's Lund. It's Paul Lund. I remember now. He's an artist, a photographer."

Slade aimed the pen at her. "Write that down. What about the other guys? The guy on the sofa with the two women? The guy behind the bar?"

"I don't remember, but if we listen to the sound we might be able to pick up more names."

They kept so quiet, Nicole could hear Slade breathing beside her. She tilted her head to concentrate on the individual voices amid the chatter. She heard her own name several times, but that was natural.

Slade grabbed her wrist. "Davey. Did you hear that?"

She replayed the previous several seconds of the

video and heard Lars's voice. "Davey, Davey, make it strong."

"You're right. That could be Dave or David. Lars always had a nickname for everyone, and I think he's talking to the guy pouring drinks."

"Okay, so we have Lars, Giles, Paul Lund and Davey." He took up the pen and scribbled the new name on the piece of paper. "There are two more men at the party—the black guy and the short one with the long hair. Do you remember them?"

"I don't remember their names. The white guy has an English accent. Can you hear him? That's not Giles." She played more of the video for him.

"Guy with English accent." Slade wrote it down. "And the other man?"

"The African-American could be an artist—sculptor, maybe. It was a very artsy bunch." She made a noise in the back of her throat when the video ended. "That's it."

"I think we went from nothing to something pretty fast, and it should be easy to locate Paul Lund."

"Then what?" She slumped in the chair and massaged the back of her neck.

"We'll find out what Lars did with that film. You know—" he'd been crouching beside her all this time and now he stood up, rolling his broad shoulders forward and back "—we keep calling this film or footage, but what physical form does it take?"

"I'm not sure. Lars used a digital camera, so he

could've copied it to any storage device. It's not on-line, though, or he would've mentioned that."

"Then it's small enough to be hidden anywhere." He gestured to the computer. "Can you find Paul Lund now?"

She scooched to the edge of her chair and flexed her fingers. A few keystrokes later, Paul Lund's website filled the screen, displaying photos of nude people—in groups.

Slade whistled. "Interesting. That's not what you all did at the party, is it?"

She rolled her eyes at him. "How could I forget he took pictures of naked people? Maybe he was doing something different two years ago."

"Yeah, these are—unforgettable. Is there an address for a gallery or contact information?"

"It doesn't look like he's big enough for a whole gallery, but there's an email address and telephone number at the bottom of the page."

"Call him."

"Me? What should I say? I haven't seen him in two years."

"Start with the truth. Ask him if he heard about Lars and see if he'll talk to you."

As she reached for the cell phone she'd brought with her into the office, Slade tapped her forearm. "Put it on speaker so I can hear, too."

She entered the number in her phone and listened

to it ring. She shrugged at Slade when Lund's voice mail picked up.

"You've reached Paul Lund. Please leave a message with your name, number and photograph number that interests you."

"Paul, this is Nicole Hastings. I'm a friend of Lars Rasmussen, and I wanted to talk to you about him. Please call me back as soon as possible."

She left her number and ended the call. "I hope he's in town."

Slade jerked a thumb at a picture of several people holding hands in a circle—sans clothing. "I don't think he needs to leave the city to find people willing to take their clothes off for art."

"I suppose not." She wrinkled her nose at the photo. "Should I contact you when he calls me back?"

"I'll wait."

She raised her eyebrows. "Here?"

"I'm staying at a hotel in Times Square. I'm not going all the way back there."

"Should we—I mean, do you want something to eat? It's after noon."

"I can just run out and get something."

Suddenly the thought of Slade Gallagher walking out that door and leaving her alone in this apartment gave her a jolt of terror. Someone had killed Giles, Lars and possibly Dahir. Was she next? Finding Lars's footage and turning it over to this Navy SEAL might be the only thing to save her life.

Unless…the guys who killed her friends found the film first. Would they leave her alone then? What about the women she'd interviewed? If the film got into the wrong hands, those women could be murdered—or worse. Whether or not the people after that footage wanted it to ID the women or not, their exposure would just be an added benefit. She owed it to the women who'd trusted her with their stories to retrieve Lars's film.

"How about it? Do you want me to get something for you, too?"

She glanced up at Slade, framed by the office door, Chanel wriggling in his arms. "We can eat here. My mom's housekeeper, Jenny, thinks it's her duty to keep the fridge stocked."

"You sure?" He rubbed Chanel behind the ear. The dog immediately stopped squirming and got the most blissful look on her face. Slade must have some magic hands.

Nicole blinked. "Of course, but I don't think Chanel's going to ever leave you alone."

"Not generally a little dog fan, but she's won me over."

"Looks like the feeling is mutual." Nicole took a step toward the door, but her phone stopped her. She looked at the display. "It's Paul."

She tapped the phone to put it on speaker and answered. "Hello?"

"Is this Nicole Hastings?" He had a more pronounced accent than Lars's, but not by much.

"Yes, Paul?"

"I got your message, and of course I'd heard about Lars. Damnedest thing. I had no idea he was suicidal. Did you? It wasn't that whole pirate thing you went through, was it?"

She raised one eyebrow at Slade. "Absolutely not. I'm finding his suicide hard to believe. Had you talked to him recently?"

"No, but I do have something for you."

"You do?" She placed a steadying hand over her heart. "What is it?"

"I'd rather show you. You're in the city?"

"Yes."

"Can you come by my studio this afternoon? It's at my loft, where I had the party. Do you remember it?"

"I do, but not the address."

Paul gave her the address of his loft studio, and they agreed to meet there in an hour.

When she ended the call, she cupped the phone in her hands. "That was easy. He's just going to turn it over to me."

"Let's hope so, and then we have to figure out why it warranted the deaths of two, possibly three, people." He set Chanel on the floor, and she promptly flopped over on her side.

Nicole walked up to the dog and nudged her paw with the toe of her sneaker. "You hypnotized her."

"Yeah, we learn that in Navy SEAL training."

She widened her eyes, and then pursed her lips. "Liar. We still have time for a quick bite to eat."

"How far are you from SoHo?"

"It's about a half hour in a taxi." She plucked her neoprene running shirt from her chest. "I'm not changing. I never ran, anyway."

"The guy takes pictures of naked people. I don't think he's going to care what you're wearing."

He hadn't moved from the doorway, so she brushed past him and wished she hadn't. She had to admit to herself that she'd been attracted to Slade from the minute she'd seen him pass by the door of the infirmary on that ship. She hadn't told the guys at the time, but she'd had a feeling he'd been the SEAL sniper who'd rescued her.

They just would've laughed at her and accused her of falling for another adventure junkie. She'd had her share of mountain climbers, skydivers, big-wave surfers and even a Wall Street trader, but a Navy SEAL topped them all.

Once her pulse returned to normal, she called over her shoulder, "Sandwich?"

"Whatever's easy. We need to head out of here soon."

She slapped together a couple of sandwiches, and they finished them on the way to the lobby.

Leo jumped into action when he saw them. "Have a good one."

"We will." Nicole almost bounded to the taxi. She couldn't wait to get her hands on that film and turn it over to the Navy or whoever would ultimately take control of it. Maybe they'd even return it to her one day so she could make that film and honor Lars and Giles.

The heavy traffic delayed them ten minutes, but Paul was waiting for them at his loft.

After introducing Slade as a friend and then shaking his hand, Paul gave her a long hug. "I can't believe our Lars is gone."

"Did he say anything to you when he left you the note for me and the footage?" She extricated herself from Paul's bear hug.

He cocked his head to the side. "Footage? I just have the photos, Nicole."

Her gaze darted to Slade and back to Paul. "Photos?"

"Of course. I thought you'd want them." He crossed the large open room, his black-and-white photographs adorning the walls. He picked up a folder from a table and raised it in the air as he strolled back to her. "These."

She flipped open the folder and bit down hard on her lip as she stared at a black-and-white photo of her and Lars, heads together, deep in conversation.

"I took those the night of the party, before we all got crazy."

She shuffled through the remaining photos with a sharp pain piercing her heart. Hugging the pictures to her chest, she asked, "Was he in New York recently?"

"He was here a few months ago. Did you miss him, too?"

"I've been in the city for just about three weeks. Does that mean you didn't see him when he was here?"

"I didn't, and that makes me very sad, especially when I think I could've done something to help him."

Slade stepped back from a collection of photos he'd been studying on the wall. "Do you know why he was in New York? Did he see any of your other friends?"

"Funding for his next project, I think." Paul tugged on his earlobe, which had several piercings. "But he did visit Dave Pullman. You might remember him. He was at the party—dark curly hair, actor."

"Davey. He was pouring the drinks." A thrill ran up her spine, but she avoided looking at Slade to share her excitement. The less Paul knew about their mission, the better.

"Davey, yes. Lars and his nicknames."

"Do you have Dave's address and phone number?" As Paul raised his pale eyebrows at her, she stammered, "I—I have something I want to give to him, something I want to share. We didn't have a chance to go to Lars's funeral or a memorial for him, so it's important for his friends to remember him."

"Exactly why I wanted to give you those pictures." He held up one finger. "One minute."

He pivoted toward his desk, which must've doubled as his office, and scooped up his phone. He tapped it a few times and read off a phone number for Dave and an address on the Lower East Side. "I'm sure Dave will be happy to see you."

"Thank you so much for the pictures, Paul."

"Absolutely." He narrowed his eyes as he looked her up and down and then turned his gaze to Slade. "Would you two be interested in doing some modeling for me?"

They both answered "no" at the same time.

Five minutes later, they stood on the sidewalk in front of Paul's building. Nicole held out the folder of pictures to Slade. "Do you mind holding these while I call Dave? I don't want them spilling out."

"They're good pictures. The guy has talent."

"Not enough to entice you to pose for him?"

"Nope."

A smile tugged on her lips as she selected Dave's number from her contacts. She'd pay good money to see a nude black-and-white photo of Slade Gallagher.

The phone rang once on the other end and then rolled into a recording. She puckered her lips and puffed out a breath. "His number's no longer in service."

"Damn. I wonder if it has anything to do with Lars."

"We still have his address. Should we pay him a visit?"

"We're close, right?"

"We could walk, or it's a ten-minute taxi ride as long as we don't get snarled in traffic—and here's one now." She raised her hand at two oncoming taxis, and the second one swerved up to the curb.

Ten minutes later, the driver dumped them off at the end of Broome, where she told him to stop. "It's easier to walk down this street."

They found Dave's building, an old brick structure squeezed between a bakery and a taco shop. Nicole placed one foot on the first step and gripped the iron railing. "If he's not there, should we wait?"

"You can leave him a note. Maybe the bakery has some paper or a napkin to write on, but give it a try."

With Slade close behind her, she stepped up on the porch and reached for the bell. Before she could press it, the door swung open and a dark-haired man carrying a bicycle on his shoulder squeezed by them.

Slade reached past her to catch the door before it closed, but something about the man's hair had her jerking her head to the side.

He'd set the bike on the sidewalk, and his eyes met hers with a flicker of recognition.

"Dave? Davey?" She descended the step and moved beside him. "I'm Nicole…"

She didn't get a chance to finish, because Davey Pullman threw his bike at her and took off running down the street.

Chapter Four

Nicole stumbled backward and landed awkwardly on the bottom step at Slade's feet with a bike on top of her.

"Are you all right?" He crouched beside her, lifting the bike from her legs.

She flailed at his arms as he tried to help her up. "Go after him. That's Dave!"

"Are you sure you're okay?"

"It's a bike, Slade. Don't let Dave get away."

Slade jumped to his feet, shoved the folder of pictures into Nicole's arms and launched down the sidewalk after the man running in the direction of the Williamsburg Bridge. Could he run across the bridge?

Dave seemed to be slowing down and probably didn't realize he had company on his jog. Then he cranked his head over his shoulder, and his mouth dropped open. He swung back around and almost ran into the path of a taxi, whose driver laid on his horn.

Slade pumped his legs harder and caught up to Dave just as he started to enter a park. He didn't want to hurt the guy, but he *had* shoved Nicole to the ground with a bike. He had to pay for that.

Slade ground his back teeth and took a flying leap at Dave. The smaller man's body folded beneath his as Slade smashed him face-first into the grass.

Panting, Slade rolled off him, keeping a knee pressed to Dave's midsection. "Why are you running? Nicole just wants to talk to you."

Dave grunted, and a few seconds later his eyes bulged from their sockets.

Slade eased up on the pressure he was applying to the man's stomach, but his knee beneath Dave's rib cage was not the reason for his bug eyes.

Nicole rolled up beside them on Dave's bike. She flicked the bell once before hopping off. "What is your problem?"

Dave finally found his voice. "I'm sorry I pushed you, but I don't want to talk to you. I don't want to be seen with you. I don't know anything."

Slade rested on his haunches next to Dave, still huffing and puffing on the ground. "Obviously you know something, or you wouldn't have taken off like that."

"And now we're talking very publicly when we could've been having a nice conversation at your place." Nicole waved her arms to take in the park. "Did Lars give you the Somalia footage or not?"

"I wouldn't take it from him. If he wanted to gal-livant all over the world getting himself in trouble, that's his business, but I didn't want any part of it."

"Why did you think taking the film from him would be trouble for you?" Slade asked.

"Are you kidding?" Dave struggled to a sitting position and pulled a pack of cigarettes out of the front pocket of his pants. "Do you mind?"

Slade shrugged, and Nicole shook her head and said, "That's why you can't run very fast."

Dave shook out the crushed package and retrieved a book of matches from his other pocket. He lit a cigarette with a trembling hand. "Lars stopped by my place with a crazy story about someone being after him. He suspected it had something to do with the film he'd shot in Somalia, because someone had broken into a place he'd been staying with a woman in San Francisco and stolen some film he had there, but the Somalia stuff wasn't there."

"Why did he connect that break-in to Somalia?" Nicole swung her leg over the bike and propped it against a park bench.

"He'd just heard about Giles, and after the theft in San Francisco, he felt like he was being followed."

Slade glanced at Nicole. She'd had the same feel-ings.

"Did you see the film Lars was trying to give you?" Slade held his breath as Dave released another stream of smoke into the air between puckered lips.

"You mean the actual footage?"

"No. The physical thing—was it on a disc or what?"

"A little disc, like this." Dave held his thumb and index finger about two inches apart.

"Did you send his letter to me?"

Nicole had perched on the edge of the bench and clasped her hands between her knees. She had a bloody scrape on her right wrist from Dave's bike, and a flare of anger surfaced in Slade's chest. The guy was a coward in more ways than one.

Dave took a long drag from his cigarette and emitted words and smoke at the same time. "I wouldn't take any of it. He wanted me to hide the disc and send the letter to you if anything happened to him."

"Do you know who sent the letter for him? Because I got it today."

"I don't know, and I don't want to know. When I heard Lars offed himself, I was damned glad I refused to help him. Lars kill himself? You ever hear of anything more ludicrous?" Dave shook his head and crushed out his smoke. "They really were out to get him and that footage. If you're smart, you'll leave it alone."

"I can't. Someone's after me, too."

Dave's head jerked up, and he pushed to his feet. "What is it with you people? Why go looking for trouble when it finds you, anyway?"

"Well, now I'm in it, and this guy—" she aimed

her finger at Slade "—is going to help me get out of it."

Was that what she thought? The pressure was really on, especially since this was an assignment way out of his comfort zone.

Slade rose to his feet and planted himself in front of Dave, in case he got any more ideas about taking off. "Who else did Lars see when he was in the city? Who else was here? We already know Paul Lund was out of town."

"Is that how you found me? Paul?"

"I was looking at video from that party at Paul's place almost two years ago. Were those all of Lars's New York friends? Are they still here? Were they here when Lars was in the city?"

"There are probably only two people from that party Lars would've contacted besides me—Andre Vincent and Trudy Waxman."

Nicole sprang to her feet and pulled her phone from the pocket of her sweatshirt. "Do you have their contact info?"

"I don't, but Andre's a sculptor. You should be able to find him, and Trudy's an actress. She's in some off-off-Broadway play right now. It's at the Gym at Judson, that church in Greenwich Village." Dave grabbed the handlebars of his bike and plucked out the folder Nicole had stashed in his basket and dropped it on the bench beside her. "Can I go now? That's all I know about it."

"Yeah, thanks." Nicole pocketed her phone. "I don't know why you had to run like that."

"Because I'm scared." Dave pushed his bike and put one foot on a pedal. Rolling forward, he turned and looked over his shoulder. "And if you were smart, you'd be scared, too."

As he rode off, Nicole plopped down on the bench again, rubbing her elbow. "Lars did a number on Dave. If he hadn't freaked him out so much, he would've been able to leave the film with him."

Slade crouched before her and took her hands. "You're injured. Does your elbow hurt, too?"

"A little." She rolled her wrist outward. "I didn't even notice that blood before."

"Let's get you back to your place and clean that up."

Tilting her head back, she cupped one hand over her eyes, shading them from the sun. "How'd you bring Dave down? Didn't anyone interfere?"

"I tackled him. There weren't that many people around. For all I know, they thought I was chasing down someone who'd lifted my wallet." He tugged a strand of her hair that had come loose from her ponytail. "And you riding in on that bike like the cavalry."

A big grin claimed her face, and he felt like a hundred suns had just come out. Nicole had those supermodel good looks, but with a bloody smudge on her arm, her messy ponytail and all those gleaming white teeth, she looked like a happy-go-lucky girl next door—a really hot girl next door.

"That was pretty cool, wasn't it?" She launched herself from the bench, practically knocking him over. "Now we need to track down Andre and Trudy."

"We'll need a computer for that, and you still need to get that cut cleaned up."

They took another taxi back to the apartment, and Chanel proceeded to paw Slade's ankles. "Does this dog ever get out?"

"My mom has a dog walker." She wagged her finger at him. "Don't ask. She comes by every morning to feed and walk Chanel and then returns at dusk."

"That's not one of your duties when you stay here?"

"My mother doesn't trust me to walk Chanel. She doesn't trust me with a lot of things."

"Really? You seem pretty competent to me."

"For chasing down guys on bikes, but not domestic things."

He preferred women who could chase down guys on bikes to those who excelled at the domestic arts. Pointing to the door off the living room that led to her small office, he asked, "How about I look up Andre and Trudy while you wash and dress that scrape?"

"I'm going to take a shower and change. Is that okay?" Tucking the folder containing Lund's photographs beneath her arm, she crossed the room to the office. "I'll get you logged in. A sculptor and an actress—I told you Lars hung with an artsy crowd."

"So your mom doesn't trust you to walk the dog?"

She glanced at him over her shoulder. "Back to that?"

"I just can't imagine someone not trusting you to follow through. You seem incredibly capable."

"Capable in the wrong way." She bumped the office door open with her hip. "According to Mom."

"Traveling to exotic and dangerous countries to expose important stories to the light of day isn't the right way?"

She powered up her computer and entered a password. "Ah, my mother would rather have me here heading up a multitude of charitable organizations she founded with my father's money. It's not an unworthy endeavor—just not me."

He pulled up a chair in front of the monitor coming to life. They had more in common than he would've thought. "I get that."

"Not many people do." She stepped back, tipping her head at the computer. "It's all yours. I'm beginning to think even if we find their phone numbers, we'd be better off coming at these people with the element of surprise."

"I think you're right." He tapped her arm above the dried blood of the cut. "You take care of that, and I'll find our friends."

"I won't be long." She swept out of the office with a flick of her fingers.

He murmured, "Capable," at her back and then turned his attention to the computer. It didn't take him long to find Andre Vincent. The sculptor's work was being featured in a series of modern art exhibits around the city, with each artist rotating among the galleries.

Slade peeled a sticky note from a pad of them and jotted down the name and address of the gallery where Andre would be visiting tonight.

Trudy Waxman was almost as easy to locate. He looked up the Gym at Judson, which had a play listed on the calendar of events for tonight. When he clicked on the cast of characters, her name popped up.

Again, he reached for a sticky note and wrote down the name and address of the theater and the play times.

A gallery and a play—he hadn't crammed this much culture into one evening since he'd been back in San Francisco and his parents had dragged him to the opera and a fund-raiser with ballet dancers after. His eye twitched at the recollection.

"Any luck?" Nicole poked her head into the office.

She'd freed her hair from its ponytail, and the strands slid over one shoulder like a smooth ribbon of caramel.

"All kinds of luck." He gestured her into the room. "Found both of them."

She sauntered into the office and leaned over his shoulder to peer at the monitor, engulfing him in a fresh scent that reminded him of newly mowed lawns.

She snorted softly. "*Glinda Fox Gets High?* That's the name of the play?"

"That's it, and Trudy doesn't even play Glinda."

"I said Lars's friends were artists. I didn't say they were particularly good ones."

"Andre's stuff doesn't look half-bad, if you like lumps of stone with faces poking out of it."

"Ugh. Sounds hideous. Where do we find these lumpen treasures?"

He stuck one of the notes to his fingertip and waved it at her. "It just so happens that some of his work is going to be on exhibit at Satchel's Gallery in Chelsea, and the artist is going to be in attendance. It's part of some revolving show for artists."

"If we go there, are we going to have time to catch Glinda getting high?"

"According to my schedule—" he attached the second note to another finger and held them both up "—we can stop in at the gallery at seven o'clock and still have time to see the play at eight, depending on what we find out from Andre."

"Maybe after talking to Andre, we won't need to sit through the play." Nicole wrinkled her nose. "We don't really have to sit through the play, do we? We can just meet her after."

"Do you have anything better to do?" His gaze swept from her bare feet with painted toes to her glossy hair, noting along the way her jeans encasing her long legs, topped off with a plain black T-shirt. She looked stylish without even trying.

"Nope, but I'd like to eat some dinner before we check out that art show."

"I need to change, anyway." He tugged on the hem of his sweatshirt. "How about we head back to my hotel in Times Square, grab a bite somewhere near there and then go to Andre's show?"

"Works for me."

He walked the chair back from the desk. "Do you want to shut down your computer?"

"That's okay. It'll go to sleep and log me out in about ten minutes. Let me put on my shoes, and I'll be ready."

He followed her from the office and flicked off the light on their way out. She'd already brought a pair of shoes and a jacket downstairs and she slid her feet into a pair of animal-print high heels that put her almost at his height, with no self-consciousness at all.

Nicole reminded him a lot of the young, wealthy women who populated his parents' circles in California—confident, self-assured and accustomed to their privilege—the type of woman he usually steered clear of.

But none of the rich girls he knew would step one foot in Somalia, or any other part of Africa, or Central America, or any of the other places Nicole had been to tell a story.

She slipped into the slim black blazer that skimmed the top of her hips and ducked beneath the strap of a small black purse that hung across her body.

"All set."

Leo was off duty, so the doorman with the second shift called a taxi for them, and Slade gave him the name of his hotel. When they got out of the taxi and made their way through the revolving door, Nicole turned to him.

"I'll just wait for you down here at the bar. Take your time."

"I won't be long." He strode toward the bank of elevators with disappointment stabbing his gut. Had he seemed too anxious to get her alone in his hotel room? He punched the button to call the car.

She had the right idea. They'd just met this morning—hardly enough time to be showering and changing in each other's presence. At her mother's place, a massive staircase and several rooms had been between them when Nicole had changed. He hadn't even heard the shower. Yeah, way too intimate too quickly.

Even though he *had* saved her life.

He raced through the shower and mimicked her

outfit with dark jeans, a black T-shirt and black motorcycle boots. He grabbed a black leather jacket on his way out of the room.

When he spotted her in the lobby bar, she was chatting with the bartender over a glass of red wine. She had one of those personalities that got people talking—necessary in her line of work, completely unnecessary in his.

He started forward, navigating through the small tables, already beginning to fill up for happy hour. He perched on the stool next to hers and tapped her wineglass. "Do you want to finish that before we find dinner?"

"I could if you'll join me." She drew her brows over her nose in a V. "That is if you *can* join me. Are you on duty or something?"

"I'm not a cop." He nodded to the bartender, who rushed over. "I'll have what she's having."

She swirled the ruby liquid in her glass. "It's just the house merlot."

"Sounds good to me."

As she held her glass to her lips, she studied him over the rim. "What *is* your function? I've never heard of the US military operating stateside."

"Some do on occasion, but this is a special assignment. Off the radar, off the books."

"So, if one of the other snipers had shot the pirate who was holding me, would he be here instead of you? Is that how the Navy made the determination?"

"I'm not exactly sure. They called. I responded." The bartender had placed his glass of wine in front of him, and he clinked it against hers. "That's how the military works."

They finished their wine over casual chatter and then walked a few blocks to a small bistro, where Nicole had a second glass of red.

At the end of dinner, she pinged her fingernail against her empty glass. "I hope I'm not going to be required to hop on a bike and chase someone down this time. I'm ready for a nap."

"Uh-oh. How are you ever going to stay awake for the play?"

"Wake me up when it's over."

They took another taxi to the gallery on West Twenty-Fourth Street, and Slade discovered this was Nicole's preferred method of transportation around the city. Her mother kept a car service on call, but Nicole had confided that she didn't like the ostentatiousness of it all, even though she seemed comfortable with most of the perks her father's wealth provided. He supposed she had to draw the line somewhere.

Fifteen minutes later, they sauntered into the gallery, a small space crammed with sculptures. Nicole saw Andre immediately and elbowed Slade in the ribs.

They feigned interest in some god-awful piece while Andre talked to a couple. When he was done, they wandered toward him until Nicole planted herself in front of him.

"Andre Vincent, right?"

"That's right." His smile dimmed a fraction as he looked into Nicole's eyes. "You're Lars's friend. The one he went to Somalia with to make that film."

"Did you hear about Lars?"

"I did, yeah. Shocking news."

"Did you see Lars when he was in the city?"

"I missed him, and now I'm sorry I did." His gaze shifted to Slade.

"This is my friend Slade."

They shook hands, and as far as Slade could tell, Andre wasn't lying about not seeing Lars. At least, he hadn't taken off in a sprint like Dave had.

Andre stroked his beard. "Was there something you wanted to ask me about Lars?"

"He left a note for me when he was in New York and gave it to someone to mail to me later." Nicole lifted her shoulders. "I was just trying to figure out who that was."

"You checked with Dave Pullman or that actress, Trudy? I don't remember her last name, but I think they saw him when he was in town."

"We checked with Dave, and we're on our way to see Trudy Waxman."

Andre snapped his fingers. "Waxman, that's it. Yeah, I'm sorry. That's crazy Lars would do that. No clue he was even depressed."

"Tell me about it." Nicole smudged a tear from the corner of her eye. "Thanks, Andre, and good luck with your show."

When Andre turned to greet a browser, Slade tapped Nicole's arm. "It's 7:40. Can we walk to the theater?"

"It's a little over a mile. If I weren't wearing these shoes, I'd say let's go for it."

"Taxi, it is."

Nicole gave a quick wave to Andre as they exited the gallery and then turned to Slade. "You believed him, didn't you? He seemed like he was telling the truth, but he could've been lying."

"That's a possibility, but he didn't seem nervous. If it doesn't pan out with Trudy, then someone's lying, or Lars has other friends you don't know."

"I hope Trudy's the one." She stepped into the street and waved down a taxi as only a New Yorker could. A few blocks from their destination, she thrust some money into the front seat. "We'll get out here."

They hustled along the sidewalk to the theater, housed in an old church, and Slade bought two tickets. As they took their seats, he brushed his lips against Nicole's ear. "If it's awful, we can always grab a cup of coffee and wait outside for her."

She winked, and the gesture seemed intimate— or he was reading way too much into her every expression.

Thirty minutes later, they were still in their seats.

The play wasn't bad, and Trudy lit up the stage every time she appeared on it. Nicole laughed in all the right places, nudging his arm as she did so, and he tried not to get too excited about it.

The sixty-minute running time didn't warrant an intermission, so at the end of the show, Slade jumped to his feet to stretch his legs. The rest of the audience joined him in a standing ovation, and the actors came out for a curtain call.

"Let's see if we can catch her in the back." Slade took Nicole's arm, and they squeezed past the people in their row and spilled onto the sidewalk with the others eager for some fresh air.

His hand inched down to hers as he led her around the back of the church. The church door opened onto a small quad, shared with another structure across the way. The actors were crossing from the church to this other building, and Slade and Nicole joined the stream of people.

Slade poked his head inside the room where the actors and their friends joked, jostled each other and passed around bottles of wine. He spotted Trudy sitting in a corner, taking off her makeup.

Gripping Nicole's shoulders, he turned her toward the actress. "She's over there. Wanna give it a try in here or wait until she's done?"

"By the looks of this bunch, we might be waiting a long time. Let's hit her up now."

Nicole squeezed past Slade into the room, and he

followed as she wended her way through the crowd. She pulled up a chair next to Trudy and touched her shoulder. "Trudy?"

Trudy finished swiping a cotton ball across one eye and then met Nicole's gaze in the mirror. Trudy's red-lipsticked mouth formed an O, and she swung around in her seat. "You're Lars's friend Nicole. Did you get the letter?"

Nicole's eyes flashed toward Slade's face before turning back to Trudy. "I did. Thank you so much."

"How did you know it was me?" Trudy grabbed a glass of wine that someone handed to her and took a swig. "Lars wanted it to be anonymous."

"Process of elimination. I looked up Lars's New York friends, and your name surfaced."

Trudy wiped a bead of sweat from her brow and took another gulp of wine. "I suppose Lars should've anticipated that. I mean, you are a journalist, right?"

"In a sense."

"Do you want some wine?" Trudy fanned her face. "It's so hot in here."

Slade stuffed his hands in the pockets of his leather jacket. Trudy must be overheated from her performance, because the cool breeze from the open door had him chilled.

"No, thanks." As she glanced over her shoulder, Nicole dipped her head closer to Trudy's. "So, did Lars tell you where to hide the film, or did you hide it? Do you know where it is?"

Trudy bit her bottom lip, still red from her heavy lipstick. "He really didn't want me to tell you…or anyone. Something *did* happen to him, didn't it? I'm sure you don't believe he killed himself any more than I do."

"I don't believe it. That's why it's important to get that film and turn it over to someone." Nicole jerked her thumb at Slade. "This is the guy. The US government is now looking for Lars's film."

Trudy's eyes popped open as she stared at Slade. "You're kidding. I thought Lars was just paranoid, but you know, I'd do anything for that guy."

Sniffing, Trudy took another hit from her wine and almost knocked the glass over when she set it down on the cluttered vanity.

"Please, Trudy." Slade crouched down next to her bouncing knees. Her nerves must've been getting to her. "I don't think Lars knew the full importance of that film, only that someone was after it. We need to know where it is. We need to make sense of Lars's death."

"I understand. I have a key. It's…" Trudy trailed off with a jerky nod. She reached for her glass again with a trembling hand. "I feel…dizzy."

Maybe she should lay off the wine. Slade put a hand on her knee. "Tell us where the film is, Trudy."

With her breath now coming out in rapid puffs, Trudy put her hand to her throat. "I don't… I don't."

A spike of adrenaline rushed up Slade's spine. "What is it? What's wrong?"

Traces of spittle at the corner of Trudy's mouth marred her red lipstick. "I can't…"

Nicole dropped beside him as she tried to take Trudy's hands, now flailing at her sides. "Slade, what's wrong with her?"

"I don't know."

As Trudy gurgled, Nicole put her ear close to the agitated woman's mouth. "Trudy? What's wrong? What can we do?"

Slade shouted, "Someone get some water."

As Nicole staggered to her feet, Trudy arched her back and slipped to the floor, foam bubbling out of her mouth. She jerked like a fish on a line.

Nicole yelled. "Water! Someone bring some water. Trudy's sick."

Slade hovered over the convulsing woman and loosened the neckline of her blouse. He kicked the chair out of the way as her writhing head came perilously close to the leg.

Suddenly, her bucking body stilled and her eyes rolled to the back of her head. She'd slipped into unconsciousness.

Taking Trudy's limp wrist between his fingers, Slade pressed his ear against her chest.

Nicole had her phone in one hand as she grabbed a bottle of water with the other from a terrified bystander. She held the water out to Slade. "Will this help?"

Slade placed Trudy's arm across her midsection. "Nothing's going to help her now. She's dead."

Chapter Five

Nicole clutched her stomach and took a step back. Her head swiveled as she took in the room, people now pressing in on her to get a look at Trudy—dead on the floor.

The responsible party had to be someone in this room. Someone who didn't want Trudy telling them the location of the film. Someone who might have a clear shot at them now.

"We have to get out of here." She tugged at Slade's arm.

He pulled his sleeve over his hand and grabbed the stem of the wineglass, putting his nose to the rim. As he set it back down on the vanity, he called out, "Anyone call 911 yet?"

"I did." A woman still in her theatrical makeup held up her phone. "Is it the epilepsy?"

"I called." A man answered from the crush of people.

"I'm a doctor." A woman pushed through and dropped to Trudy's inert form. "Is she conscious?"

"I don't think so." Slade jimmied out of the circle that had formed around Trudy and nodded to Nicole.

She got it. He wouldn't want to be caught here. He might even be under strict orders to keep a low profile. She stumbled from the circle herself, crouching and weaving her way through the jam of people as a siren wailed beyond the church's courtyard.

When she reached the door, Slade grabbed her arm and strode toward the church. The adrenaline flooding her system kept her legs pumping as she matched him step for step.

He steered her along the side of the church and out to the front, where the first emergency vehicle was pulling up to the curb. Hunching into his leather jacket, Slade veered to the right and away from the first responders.

Her heels clicked on the cement as she kept up with him, her fingers hooked in the back pocket of his jeans. They walked this way for about two blocks, silently, until Slade took a detour into an ice cream shop.

He pointed to a high table for two at the back of the shop, away from the window. "Let's sit."

Her feet didn't need a second invitation, and she perched on the edge of the chair, kicking off her shoes. "Trudy was murdered."

"Excuse me. Are you going to buy something?" The clerk behind the counter squinted and shoved his glasses up the bridge of his nose. "There's no table service."

"Hold that thought." Slade rapped his knuckles on the table in front of her, and he approached the counter. "Raspberry gelato, double scoop, two spoons."

He waited at the counter, back stiff, clutching some money in his fist, while the clerk scooped up the gelato. Slade exchanged the money for the dessert and stuffed the change in his front pocket.

When he returned to the table, he shoved the little cup of purplish-pink gelato in her direction.

She glanced down at it and saw the color of Trudy's cheeks instead. "How did they get to her?"

"It could've been the wine." He jabbed one of the spoons into the mound of gelato.

"I saw you smelling the glass. Did you notice anything?"

"Smelled like wine to me, but whatever she drank could've been colorless and odorless."

She put a hand over her mouth. "If it was the wine, then it was someone there, in the room. It had to be."

"Since nobody else dropped dead, I'm assuming someone targeted her glass—and saw us talking to her."

"Why would the people after the film want to kill her? They could've questioned her. No matter how loyal she was to Lars, Trudy would've given up the film to save her life."

He rubbed his knuckles against the sandy-blond scruff on his chin. "Next best thing to finding the film would be that it stays hidden and nobody else finds it. If someone happens to stumble across it, he or she wouldn't understand the significance of it. Hell, we might not understand the significance of it."

"That's if it stays hidden." She hunched across the small table, her nose almost touching his. "Trudy mentioned a key. Remember? She said she had a key."

Slade reached into the inside pocket of his jacket and withdrew a key chain, dangling it from his index finger.

Nicole's jaw dropped. "Is it hers? How did you get that?"

"In the confusion, when all eyes were on the doctor and I was sniffing the wineglass, I noticed Trudy's purse. I figured if she had any keys, they'd be in her bag, so I reached inside and snagged them."

Curling her fingers around the set of keys, Nicole asked, "Do you think the key she mentioned is one of these?"

"That's what I was hoping, but we have no idea what type of key Trudy was talking about. It could be a key to a safe-deposit box or a safe in her apartment, or a key to something we may never locate." Slade scraped a plastic spoon across the little mountain of gelato and shoved it in his mouth.

She dropped the key chain, which was the letter

T, on the table with a clatter and spread out the five keys. She nudged the first one. "This looks like an apartment key, right?"

"Probably."

"But so does this." She tapped the second key on the ring. "This one looks like it would fit a padlock, and this one a bike lock."

"That one is some kind of locker key." He aimed his spoon at a short, stubby key with blue plastic on the top.

Pinching the key between two fingers, Nicole brought it close to her face and squinted at the raised writing on the plastic. "Just numbers, no location."

"Is there any place in the city that still has lockers? I know the airports and the train stations haven't had them for years."

"I took someone to the Statue of Liberty recently, and she had to put her backpack in a locker before going up, but I can't remember if those had keys or were electronic." Nicole ran the tip of her finger along the key's ridges and grooves. "How are we going to find out where this key belongs?"

"By using this key." Slade plucked one of the apartment keys from bunch and jiggled the ring in front of her face.

"We're going to break into Trudy's apartment?"

"It's not breaking in if we have a key."

"A key we stole."

"A key Trudy died protecting."

Nicole huffed out a breath and massaged her right temple with two fingers. "I'm exhausted."

"Have some." In the space between them, Slade held out a spoon piled high with purple gelato.

She opened her mouth like a baby bird, and he placed the plastic utensil against her tongue. She closed her lips around it and sucked the gelato into her mouth. As the tart, cold flavor invaded her taste buds, she squeezed her eyes shut.

When she opened her lids, her gaze met Slade's stare, his black pupils rimmed with the intense blue of his irises. "Are the police going to wonder about Trudy's keys? Are they going to wonder about the couple talking to her at the time of her collapse?"

"Probably. Did you know anyone there?"

"No."

"The scene was chaotic. I'm sure an autopsy will be ordered, since women Trudy's age don't typically fall into seizures and die, but the cops may not suspect foul play. And if they don't, they might not take that wineglass into evidence."

"I heard someone say something about epilepsy. Do you think this is just a coincidence?"

"No."

Nicole pushed the cup of gelato away, suddenly feeling sick to her stomach. "Who gave her the wine?"

"I didn't notice." He scooped up the keys and bobbled them in his palm. "But we're going to find out where Trudy lived and do a thorough search of her place."

"What if she has a roommate?"

"We'll deal with that when we get to it, and we'd better do it soon. If the autopsy shows poison, the police will want to search her place, too."

Nicole pressed her palms against her temples. "This is too much for me to think about right now. I just want to go home, back to my mom's place."

"Is the building secure? Have there ever been any break-ins?"

Her heart did a double-time beat in her chest. "Not that I know of. Mom's never mentioned any. You don't think I'm safe there?"

"I broke in the back way, didn't I? Got to your mail. Nobody stopped me."

"Thanks for pointing that out." She folded her arms and dug her fingers into her biceps.

"I was sent here specifically to protect you, Nicole, and I plan to do that. I'm staying with you tonight at your mom's place."

A little thrill fluttered through her body that had as much to do with the thought of having this SEAL spending the night with her as it did being under his protection.

She smoothed her hands down the thighs of her jeans while she tried to paste a nonchalant expression on her face. The warmth that surged in her cheeks just told her she'd failed. She grabbed a spoon and shoved a glob of half-melted gelato in her mouth.

She talked around the sweet raspberry taste. "If you think it's necessary."

With the last word, a drop of gelato dribbled from the corner of her mouth. As her tongue darted out to catch it, Slade's finger shot out to dab it from her lip and she wound up licking the tip of his finger.

They both said, "Sorry," at the same time.

She grabbed a napkin from the dispenser. "Just goes to show you how tired I am."

"Then let's get out of here." He lifted the cup by the rim between two fingers. "Do you want any more of this?"

"No." She'd probably end up wearing it down the front of her T-shirt.

He dumped the cup in the trash, and they snagged a taxi a half block away.

When they got to the apartment on the Upper East Side, Slade seemed to vibrate with electricity. His body tensed up and his head swiveled from side to side. The hand on her back became insistent as he guided her past the doorman and into the lobby of the building.

He jerked his head toward one corner of the lobby. "Camera there. Does anyone get past the doorman?"

"Not if they don't live here or aren't with someone who does. The doormen know all of the residents."

Slade nodded as if ticking off items on an internal checklist. As they entered the elevator, he tilted back his head. "Cameras in here, too."

"Feel better now?"

"Makes it more secure, but not impenetrable—nothing is."

"You're just full of good news tonight."

When they stepped inside the apartment, Chanel greeted them by spinning around and dancing on her hind legs.

Slade picked her up. "Does she need to go out?"

"Livvy, the dog walker, was already here, and believe it or not, my mother trained Chanel to use a litter box. It's in the laundry room. She'll be good until tomorrow morning." She pointed at the ceiling. "There are a few rooms up there. You can take your pick."

He shrugged out of his leather jacket and dropped it over the back of the sofa. "I'm going to bunk down here. I'd rather be close to the front door than tucked away in some bedroom with the door shut."

Nicole eyed her mother's white brocade couch, threaded with gold, and shrugged. Mom let Chanel sleep on it, why not a six-foot-two Navy SEAL protecting her daughter?

"I'll get you a blanket and a pillow. There's a half bathroom down here, and I'll find a toothbrush and some toothpaste for you. Anything else?"

"Soap and a towel in there?"

"Yeah. Be right back." She took the stairs two at a

time and threw open a cupboard in the hallway. She pulled a blanket from the bottom shelf and ducked into one of the bedrooms to drag a pillow from the bed.

She made a stop at the bathroom connected to her bedroom and found a new toothbrush, still in its packaging. She balanced it on top of the folded blanket and pillow as she carefully descended the staircase.

Slade glanced up from scratching Chanel behind the ear and patted the sofa cushion beside him. "Am I going to have to share my bed with her?"

"I'm afraid so." *Lucky girl.*

She dumped the blanket and pillow next to him, retaining the toothbrush in her hand. She waved it in the air. "Brand-new."

"Thanks. I'm sure Chanel and I will manage."

"Oops, I forgot the toothpaste." She bent forward to place the toothbrush on the coffee table, but it ended up on the floor as her hand jerked. "Where did that gun come from?"

"My hotel room. I had it in my jacket pocket." He traced a finger along the handle. "A little smaller than I'm used to, but it'll do."

"I didn't realize you had a gun with you."

"How else am I supposed to protect you? Does it bother you?"

"I've seen plenty of guns—big ones—up close and personal on my travels. Our translators, including Dahir, used to carry weapons. As long as it's not pointing at me, I can handle it."

"Do you want me to get the toothpaste? Just tell me where it is. You don't need to go running up and down the stairs for me."

"It's the least I can do for you and your…gun." She spun around and called over her shoulder as she jogged up the stairs, "Do you need anything else?"

"We're fine."

She took a used tube of toothpaste from her mother's bathroom and paused to study her flushed face and glittering eyes in the mirror. She was accustomed to a certain level of danger when she went on assignments. Now that danger had followed her home. Did she have to look so…thrilled about it? Her mother was probably right about her. She'd never settle down.

She dismissed the woman in the mirror and glided back down the stairs.

Slade had gotten rid of Chanel, along with his boots and socks. With one bare foot resting on the opposite knee, he was checking his phone.

"Here's the toothpaste."

"Thanks, Nicole." He held up his phone. "Looks like the news about an off-off-Broadway actress dying after a performance is out."

"Do you think they would've killed her if we hadn't contacted her?"

"Yes, and don't think we led them to her, either. If

that wine was poisoned, it was spiked before we got there. They were either determined to get the location of the film out of her, or wanted to make sure that she wouldn't pass the info along to someone else."

The events of the day seemed to hit Nicole all at once, and her shoulders sagged beneath the weight of all the recent deaths. "I'm calling it a day. Hope you sleep well, but not too well. I wouldn't want you to miss someone trying to break into the place."

He saluted. "Chanel and I are on the job."

She turned a dubious eye on the little dog, who'd returned to Slade's side, curled into a fluffy ball next to his gun. Her mom would have a fit if she could see her precious pup now.

"'Night, Slade."

"Good night," he called out, his voice muffled as he shook out the blanket.

Nicole plodded up the stairs and got ready for bed in slow motion, exhaustion seeping into every muscle of her body.

As she crawled between the sheets, her phone, which was charging on her nightstand, buzzed. She reached over and swiped her finger across the display to wake it up and then entered her pass code. A text from an unknown sender popped up, and she read it aloud.

"'Heard about Trudy. I'm outta here.'"

Must be Dave. She didn't blame him.

She plugged her phone back in and burrowed into her pillow.

She might be out of here, too, if she didn't have a hot Navy SEAL on guard in her living room.

Chapter Six

The following morning, Nicole woke up to find that the hot Navy SEAL could also make coffee. She trailed downstairs, yawning and inhaling the scent of freshly brewed java.

He raised a cup of the stuff in her direction as she wedged a shoulder against the arched entrance to the kitchen. "Just in time."

"You know your way around a kitchen."

"I know my way around a coffeepot, although the gadgets on this one could rival the control panel of a Blackhawk helicopter."

"Is that coffee black? Because I like mine with lots of soy milk."

"Soy milk?" He shook his head as he opened the fridge door. "How do you manage to get by in some of those primitive locales you frequent without soy?"

"When in Rome." She shrugged. "I can make do when I have to. I'm really not high maintenance, despite my current surroundings."

"I already figured that out." He placed the coffee cup and a carton of vanilla soy on the granite island in the middle of the kitchen. "You wouldn't have lasted two minutes in some of the countries you visited if you were high maintenance."

She pulled up a stool and parked herself at the island. Pouring the soy into the coffee, she watched it fan out in gentle circles until the black liquid turned toffee. She inhaled the sweet vanilla as she took a careful sip.

"I can manage a basic breakfast, too, if you have some eggs."

"I don't usually eat breakfast unless I go out, but help yourself. I'm sure Jenny stocked eggs in the fridge." She warmed her hands on the mug. "What's the plan today? Are we going to search Trudy's place?"

"Once we find out where it is. Do you think Dave knows her address?"

"Uh, yeah, about Dave." She hooked her bare feet around the legs of the stool. "He sent me a text last night. I guess he heard the news about Trudy, and I don't think we're going to get another crack at him."

"Can I see the text? How do you know it's from him?"

She hunched her shoulders to her ears as an insidious trickle of fear dripped down her spine. "Just the context of the message. He said he'd heard about Trudy's death and he was out of here."

"I'm going to start my eggs." He pulled open the fridge door and continued talking with his head stuffed inside. "And you can run up and get your phone."

"Aye, aye, captain." She unwound her legs from the stool and shuffled across the cool tile. Slade pretended to be all easygoing, but he was really quite bossy.

She took the stairs two at a time as if she were on a mission. She swiped the phone from its charger on her nightstand and studied the text message on her way downstairs to make sure she hadn't missed some sinister subtext.

She stood at Slade's shoulder as he cracked an egg with one hand into a bowl. She held the phone in front of his face. "This is it. Pretty straightforward…don't you think?"

He squinted, moving his lips as if trying to decipher some ancient code. "I suppose. Wouldn't make much sense for anyone else to send a message like that."

"You mean like Trudy's killers?" She yanked back the phone and tossed it onto the counter.

"We can't rule out the possibility that they might try to reach out to you one way or another."

"That's why you're here, isn't it? In case they try to reach out to me?"

"That's right."

She could live with that. Rubbing her chin, she asked, "How'd you sleep last night?"

"Chanel and I slept great." He dumped the egg mixture into a skillet of sizzling butter.

"Did she sleep with you on the sofa?"

"All night."

"Sorry about that. At least you're not allergic." Nicole twisted her head over her shoulder. "Where is the little rascal?"

"Back on the sofa. Where else? Does she need to go out this morning?"

"She does. I usually take her out before Livvy gets here for the morning walk."

"Do you feed her in the morning?" He scuffed the eggs off the bottom of pan with a plastic spatula into fluffy mounds.

"Livvy does that after the walk."

He lifted one eyebrow. "I thought you were staying here to take care of the dog while your mom was gone."

"Not really." She picked up the fork on the counter and jabbed a clump of scrambled eggs. "If I weren't here, my mom would be boarding Chanel, but that doesn't mean she'd completely dismiss the dog sitter in favor of me. I told you before, Mom doesn't trust me with that sort of thing."

He shoved the plate of eggs toward her and she shook her head and held out the fork to him.

"Any reason in particular? Did your mother come

home one time and find Chanel's fur tangled? Paws dirty? Teeth unbrushed?"

She laughed and took a swig of coffee. "Mom just knows I'm busy, and come to think of it, if we're going to be chasing around the city looking for that film footage, I might just have Livvy take Chanel with her. I hate leaving the dog home alone all day."

"Is she much of a watchdog?" He loaded up his fork with eggs. "I mean, she didn't even curl her lip at me."

"She doesn't have a vicious bone in her body, and I really have to take her out now." She whistled. "Chanel!"

The little dog came careening around the corner of the kitchen and slid across the tiles, stopping only when she hit Slade's ankles.

"She's ready, but I'll tell you what." Slade waved his fork in the air. "Why don't you get dressed, and I'll take Chanel outside."

She sucked in the side of her cheek. "You're worried about me going outside on my own?"

"You said it yourself, Chanel's no watchdog. It'll give me a chance to sort out the neighborhood."

"In case you haven't figured it out already, this is a very good neighborhood."

"No doubt, but I want to suss out the lay of the land, take a look at the building. When I was watching you the other night, it was dark outside. I didn't get a sense if someone would be able to scale the walls or reach your windows from the outside."

"That would be nearly impossible. We're on the tenth floor."

"Nothing's impossible. Someone got to Trudy."

Nicole threw a quick glance over her shoulder as if expecting someone to come charging through the front door. "The leash is hanging on a hook inside the closet in the foyer."

"Does she have a preferred route?"

"There's a small square with a patch of grass about half a block down. You don't have to go all the way to Central Park. Livvy will take her there later."

"Maybe you can start making some calls to Paul Lund or Dave, or maybe not Dave, and see if you can get Trudy's address, or do a computer search."

"Okay, I'll get on that. You don't have to take Chanel far."

"Don't worry. I won't be long."

Did he think she was scared to be on her own in her mom's apartment in broad daylight? "I just meant, she's a small dog, small legs. It doesn't take much to exercise her."

"I'll remember that."

She left Slade eating his eggs, still dressed in all black from the night before—the disastrous night before. Would the people looking for that footage really have gotten to Trudy if they hadn't led them to her?

Once in her bedroom, Nicole opened her walk-in

closet and leaned against the doorjamb. "What do you wear to a break-in?"

Of course, as Slade had pointed out, they had Trudy's keys. Would the police be there? Had Trudy's death been categorized as a murder? What else? Twentysomething women didn't just drop dead after theatrical performances…unless they were ill.

Nicole showered quickly, deciding on a pair of boyfriend-cut jeans, a loose T-shirt and running shoes—in case they needed to make a quick getaway.

Slade hadn't returned from walking the dog, so Nicole headed to the office and fired up her computer. She did a search for Trudy Waxman and came across a small news item about her death at the theater. The article didn't mention murder.

She spun her phone toward her on the desk and sent a text to Paul Lund. Dave Pullman would probably refuse to answer even if he did have Trudy's address.

When she heard the key scrape in the lock, she jumped to her feet and hung behind the office door until she saw Slade emerge from the foyer with Chanel at his heels. She let out a small, measured breath.

"How'd it go?"

"We met a chocolate Lab, a pug and a mutt." He swooped up Chanel in his arms and unclipped her leash. "She seemed most taken with the mutt. Loves those bad boys, I guess."

Starting forward, Nicole brushed away the prickles of heat from her cheeks. Slade Gallagher couldn't be referring to himself. He was no bad boy, with his surfer good looks and easy acceptance of all her mother's high-end accoutrements.

"That mutt is Charlie, and they're already good friends. Did Charlie's owner, Emma, wonder what you were doing with Chanel?"

"I told her I was your friend and had offered to walk Chanel around the neighborhood."

"Great. I'm going to have some explaining to do when my mom comes home. Emma is just about the nosiest person on the block."

"I'm sure you'll think of something." He opened the closet door and slipped the leash over the hook. "Did you have any luck with Trudy's address?"

"Couldn't find anything online, but I also texted Paul Lund. No answer yet." She sank to an ottoman and crossed her legs beneath her. "There was an item online about Trudy, but there was nothing about murder."

"It'll take the coroner's office a few weeks to get a toxicology report if there's no apparent cause of death."

"If the NYPD doesn't suspect foul play, will the police even go to her apartment?"

"I'm not sure. If the police don't suspect murder, they probably won't search Trudy's place, but they may talk to anyone who lives there with her."

"And if she does have roommates? How are we going to get around them to search the place?"

"Let's find her place first. If there are any roommates there, we'll deal with them. You knew Trudy, sort of, or at least you knew Lars. If we get caught, we can use that as an excuse."

It took Paul Lund another hour to text her back, but when he did it was good news.

"Bingo." Nicole held up her phone to Slade, stretched out on the floor, playing with Chanel. That dog was going to miss Slade when he returned to being a SEAL, and Chanel wasn't the only one.

Slade turned his head to the side, one furry paw planted on his cheek. "He sent the address?"

"Her place is in Brooklyn."

"Did he mention anything else?"

"No. He doesn't know she's dead."

"Makes you wonder how Dave found out so quickly. Unless you were searching for Trudy's name, her death didn't exactly make prime-time news."

She snapped her fingers. "You answered your own question. Once Dave knew we were looking for Andre and Trudy, he was probably expecting something bad to happen to them—and he didn't have to wait long."

"How long does it take to get to Brooklyn and how are we getting there?"

"We can take the train. It won't take too long, less

than an hour." She tapped her phone. "I know this neighborhood, full of film school hipsters, and unless Trudy had better gigs than that off-off-Broadway play last night, I can guarantee you she has roommates."

"Unless she has rich parents."

She studied Slade as he tossed Chanel's plush toy across the room for signs of sarcasm or snarkiness, but his strong, honest face didn't show signs of either. He puzzled her, and she wanted to find out more about him personally, but how did one ask one's bodyguard about the private details of his life?

He liked dogs—that much she knew—and they liked him. Who wouldn't?

Flicking some dog hair from the front of her T-shirt, she shrugged. "Do we go over now or should we wait?"

"Let's go, since we don't know what we're going to find there."

The bell at the front door made them both twitch and sent Chanel into a tizzy.

"That has to be Livvy. Leo knows to let her up." Nicole scooted off the ottoman and then hesitated at the front door as Slade hovered behind her, his warm breath on the back of her neck. Licking her lips, she hooked the chain and inched open the door.

"It's just me." Livvy stepped back from the crack in the door and spread her arms.

Nicole swung open the door. "Right on time. Chanel's going to be starving. She had a busy morning."

Livvy stepped into the room and inclined her head when she saw Slade. Her light blue eyes did a quick assessment of the man in front of her, and she must've liked what she saw. She dimpled and held out her long fingers. "Hello, there. I'm Livvy, the dog sitter."

"Slade, the out-of-town friend." He took Livvy's hand and returned the smile, not looking lethal at all.

"I think those are the only kinds of friends Nicole has—out-of-town ones." Livvy swept up Chanel and met her nose to nose. "Hello, gorgeous."

"We already let her out for a quick walk this morning."

"Okay, I'll feed her and take her out for a longer walk to the park."

Nicole opened the door and poked her head in the hallway. "No other charges today?"

"Not today. Chanel has me all to herself." Livvy shook the little dog gently.

"You should see it when Livvy's walking four or five dogs at once—a true art." Nicole took a few steps backward and grabbed her purse from the coffee table. "We were just on our way out."

Livvy leaned forward, allowing the dog to scramble from her arms. "Before you go out, can I ask a favor?"

"Of course."

"It's colder than when I set out this morning. Can I borrow a jacket for my walk?"

"You can wear that blazer draped over the chair, or I have an NYU hoodie in the coat closet in the foyer."

"Thanks, I'll take the hoodie. That blazer looks— expensive." Livvy wiggled her fingers in the air. "Have fun."

When they got to the elevator, Slade turned to her. "Does she make a living as a dog sitter?"

"I know what my mom pays her, so I can believe it. She has a lot of high-end clients."

"I need a job when I retire from the Navy. Maybe I should look into dog sitting."

In the elevator car, she bumped his shoulder with her own. "You'd be great, and all the society matrons would love you."

"Ah, society matrons."

She pounced on his words. "Sounds like you know the breed."

"Very well."

The doors opened onto the lobby and she lost her chance to ask what he meant as Leo greeted them with a wave. "Did you see Livvy? I sent her up."

"She's all set. She'll be taking Chanel for a walk in about thirty minutes."

Leo held open the door. "Taxi?"

"Actually—" Nicole pivoted on her toes, changing direction "—we'll go out the back way. Mail come?"

"It did."

"Then I'll pick it up on the way out. Thanks, Leo."

"Have a good one."

She led Slade back to the mailboxes, even though he knew exactly where they were. She opened hers and peeked inside, holding her breath.

"You look worried. Anything unexpected?"

She flicked through the envelopes and ads. "Nothing. I'm going to leave it here."

They slipped outside into the alley between her mother's building and another high-rise. The wind whipped through the space and she zipped up her jacket. "Livvy wasn't kidding. It's chilly out here."

"I need to stop by my hotel again on the way and change clothes. I did have a shower at your place, but I could use a clean shirt."

"We can make a stop."

"You can wait in the lobby again…or come on up this time."

Forty minutes later, she wished she'd chosen the lobby as Slade peeled off his black T-shirt and tossed it on the bed.

She averted her gaze from his solid muscles by squinting at her phone. The guy was just too good to be true, and too hard to resist. He probably didn't feel the same connection to her as she did to him. He'd saved her life on that boat in the Gulf of Aden, but he'd probably rescued a lot of people. While that moment had been indelibly impressed upon her mind, it was all in a day's work for him.

He crouched in front of a suitcase in the corner

of the room, his back and shoulders flaring up from the waistband of his black jeans. Nicole swallowed and wandered to the window.

"Nice view." Times Square below barely registered on her brain.

Slade rose to his feet and turned around, a blue T-shirt clutched in one hand. "Yeah, it's great. That view is also how I know the military is not funding this little operation."

"Not the Navy?" She crossed her arms. "Who, then?"

"Some organization deep in the intelligence community. My superior officer won't even tell me, but I was specifically requested for this assignment. One of my team members was put on a similar assignment last month."

"Are they related?"

He pulled the T-shirt over his head, thank God, and then skimmed his palm over the top of his short sandy-blond hair. "Someone must think so."

"Do you?"

"There's a guy—" he ran a knuckle across the scruff on his chin "—and I'm only telling you this because you're involved and have been involved in matters in the Middle East. He started as a sniper and got on our radar during the conflict in Afghanistan, but he's branched out and may be running his own organization. We think he might've been involved in your kidnapping and in these follow-up killings."

"For what reason?" The gears of her mind had already started whirring. This would make a hell of a story.

"A broader terror organization. He'd been planning an attack in Boston last month, and someone we rescued from Pakistan a few years ago was targeted because he unwittingly had information about the plan."

"The attack at the symposium held at the JFK Library?"

"That's the one."

She pressed one hand against the glass of the window, feeling dizzy. "What would he have to do with a story about the women's movement in Somalia?"

"We don't have a clue—right now. Hoping Lars's footage can clarify that."

"Then we'd better get moving."

Slade sat on the edge of the bed and pulled off one motorcycle boot. "I'm changing shoes."

She kicked out her sneakered foot. "In case we have to make a run for it?"

"Are you sure you don't want to wait here? You'd be safe."

"I thought I was your ticket to Trudy's apartment. At least I had met her once or twice before. I doubt some woman is going to trust you, especially after her roommate just dropped dead."

"That's right, but if you don't want to go you don't

have to go." He tied his Converse and stamped his feet on the carpet as he stood up.

"Oh, I want to go."

He reached into the closet and pulled a gray sweatshirt from a hanger, the other hangers clacking in protest.

"You could be living in the lap of luxury and safety on the Upper East Side, attending charity balls and golf tournaments."

She tilted her head to one side. "You sound like you know that world well. Why?"

"I'm from it."

During their forty-minute trip to Brooklyn, Nicole grilled Slade about his background, which wasn't all that different from her own—except his upbringing had played out against the backdrop of a wealthy beach community in Orange County, California.

"So who's your father going to get to take over his business since you've opted out?"

"His business, his problem."

The set of his jaw indicated that his father had tried to make it Slade's problem, too.

"But still, your parents must be incredibly proud of what you do, who you are."

"Would you say your mother is proud of your chosen field?"

"Oh, that?" She waved her hand. "No, but I don't run around saving people's lives."

"Really?" He stretched out his legs and tapped

his feet together. "'Cause I've seen your films, and you come pretty damned close to doing just that with your exposés."

A little glow warmed a spot in her heart. "Thanks, but it doesn't come close to what you do, and my mom just thinks I'm crazy."

"Same."

The train swayed, and her shoulder bumped his. He didn't move away and neither did she. She pressed against him and felt more than his solid presence in her life right now. She felt a connection, a kindred spirit.

She'd dated plenty of wealthy guys, and they'd always sided with her mother. She'd also dated guys who were dead broke, and most of them had a hard time figuring her out. Slade got it—got her.

After the train arrived at the station in Brooklyn, they emerged onto a busy sidewalk. "Are you up for a walk? There's no subway deeper into Greenpoint."

"Let's walk. I need to stretch my legs."

Fifteen minutes later, as they turned onto Trudy's street, Slade said, "At least there are no cop cars out front."

"So, either they already came and went, or they aren't even considering homicide."

Slade took her arm at the bottom of the steps. "You got this?"

"If there's a roommate, I'm going to tell her that

Trudy had something of Lars's to give me, and I'm there to pick it up."

Slade tried the front door of the building, but it didn't budge.

"The key's probably on Trudy's key chain."

"But if there's a roommate, she's gonna wonder why we didn't just buzz." He pressed the button next to Trudy's apartment number.

The speaker crackled to life. "Yes?"

Slade mouthed an expletive while Nicole leaned into the speaker. "I'm looking for Trudy Waxman."

An audible gasp whooshed through the speaker. "A-are you a friend?"

"A friend of a friend—Lars Rasmussen."

"Lars, yes." The woman sniffed. "I'm sorry, I have some bad news…why don't you come up?"

The door buzzed and clicked, and Slade pushed it open. "Ready?"

"I guess so, but how are we going to search the place with a roommate hanging around?"

"We're going to have to get in when the room-mate's gone. In a way, it makes it easier. We know what we're dealing with instead of being surprised in the act."

They trudged up the three flights of stairs and knocked on the door of number 311.

A woman with a red-tipped nose cracked open the door. Her eyes widened when she spotted Slade hovering behind Nicole. "C'mon in."

Nicole figured she'd get right to the point. "What's the bad news?"

"Trudy passed away last night after a performance."

Nicole clapped a hand over her mouth as Slade squeezed her shoulder. "How?"

"Not sure yet, but it looks like it was her epilepsy."

"Epilepsy?" Nicole's mouth dropped open—for real this time. So she had heard right last night. "I didn't know she had epilepsy."

"Well, you weren't really her friend, were you? What's your name?"

"Nicole Hastings." She and Slade believed it would be best to stick to the truth, since Trudy might have mentioned her.

"That's right. You worked with Lars. I'm Marley."

Slade asked, "Is that the official cause of death?"

Marley's gaze darted to Slade.

"I'm sorry." Nicole tugged on the sleeve of Slade's sweatshirt. "This is my friend Steve."

Marley shook Slade's hand. "I don't know if it's official or not, but the cops came by here last night when one of Trudy's cast mates gave him our address. He told me she'd had a seizure and had passed before the EMTs even got there."

"That's horrible. I'm so sorry." Nicole touched the other woman's shoulder. "Now I feel sort of stupid being here."

"Why did you come?" Marley dabbed a shredded tissue to her nose.

"Trudy told me that Lars had given her something for me."

"Oh." Marley opened her arms to encompass the cluttered room. "What was it?"

"That's the thing." Nicole lifted one shoulder. "I don't know. Trudy didn't tell me."

"That's...strange." Marley bit her lip. "If I come across anything, I'll let you know. Trudy's sister is coming out in a few weeks to collect her things, and I'll let her know, too."

"Thanks, I appreciate it." Nicole took a half turn around the room. Did Trudy have her own room here? "Nice place. How many bedrooms?"

"We have two bedrooms and one bathroom. I'm going to have to find another roommate, but I can't even think about that right now." Marley's eyes welled with tears.

"I'm so sorry." Nicole patted Marley's arm. "We'll get out of your way."

"That's okay. A bunch of us are going out later to celebrate her life." Marley cocked her head to the side. "That's weird, isn't it?"

"What?" Nicole's heart skipped a beat. Was Marley suspicious about the epilepsy story?

"I mean, Trudy told me about Lars...about his suicide, and now she's dead, too."

"Both too young."

"Well, I can understand why you'd want something from Lars. I'll let you know if I find something."

Nicole gave Marley her cell phone number, and they said their goodbyes.

Slade waited until they hit the sidewalk before speaking. "We're going to wait until Marley goes out, and then we're going back in."

"Did you see that place? It's crammed with stuff. We'll never find it—whatever *it* is."

Slade tugged on a lock of her hair. "I didn't think you'd give up so quickly."

"I'm not giving up." A spark of heat flared in her chest. "I'm all for doing a search."

"That's what I want to hear." He pointed to a coffee place across the street. "Let's hang out over there, keep an eye on Marley's building and make our move."

They got their coffee and settled at a table by the window with a clear view of the apartment.

Nicole popped the lid from her cup and slurped the vanilla-scented foam from her latte. "How did Trudy's killers know she had epilepsy?"

"Good question. Maybe they broke into her place earlier, searched through her stuff and found her medication. They formulated a plan from that. I should've known it wouldn't be straight poison that killed Trudy. None of these deaths looks like murder."

"And who would know to connect them except me?" She took another sip of coffee and glanced over her shoulder at the sandwiches in the refrigerated case. "How long do you think we'll be waiting?"

"Who knows? We couldn't ask her what time the friends were getting together without sounding too suspicious. Marley already thought it was strange that you didn't know what Trudy had for you."

"You're right." She dug into her purse for her phone. Might as well check some emails. They could be here until nighttime. "Wow, looks like I've missed a bunch of calls."

"I think you have time to return them. Like you said, we could be here for a while."

"They're all from Livvy. I hope Chanel's okay. If anything happened to that dog on my watch, my mom would disinherit me." She touched her phone to return Livvy's call.

Livvy didn't waste any time. "Nicole, where have you been? I got hit by a car and it was hit-and-run— the bastards."

"Oh, my God. Are you all right?"

"I'm at the hospital now, waiting for X-rays. I may have broken my foot or my ankle. All I know is I can't walk on it and it hurts like hell. Don't worry about Chanel. She escaped unscathed. I can't say the same about your sweatshirt, though. That thing's trashed."

A chill zigzagged down Nicole's spine. "That's right. You borrowed my sweatshirt."

"It has a rip and some oil stains on it now, sorry. Now I'm really glad I didn't wear that blazer. My partner, Andi, picked up Chanel and took her back to our place. I hope that's okay."

"That's fine. D-did you see the car that hit you?"

"Came out of nowhere. I would've been dead if Chanel hadn't seen another dog, making me cross the street faster."

"Do you need anything?"

"Andi's taking care of everything. Just give her a call when you're ready to get Chanel. We have two other dogs at our place now, so we can handle her."

When Nicole got off the phone with Livvy, Slade was staring at her, eyebrows raised.

"Livvy got hit by a car, walking my mom's dog and wearing my sweatshirt."

Slade nodded once. "It's your turn now."

Chapter Seven

Hearing him say aloud what she'd already acknowledged to herself sent a new river of chills cascading through her body. "Livvy said the car came at her out of nowhere. All she saw was a dark blur."

"They must've been waiting for you outside and you got lucky when we decided to go out the back way. Livvy is tall and thin like you. Wearing your sweatshirt—" he snapped his fingers "—she was a dead ringer for you."

"Really bad choice of words." She hugged herself, sort of wishing Slade's arms were holding her instead of her own flimsy limbs.

"I take it Livvy is okay, since you were having a conversation with her."

"Better than Trudy." Nicole swirled her lukewarm coffee. "She may have broken her foot or ankle."

"Chanel?"

"Probably saved Livvy's life by chasing after another dog. Pulled her away from receiving the brunt of the car's force. Livvy's partner and roommate took Chanel home with her."

Slade drummed his fingers on the table. "The people after the footage are still trying to make these deaths appear like accidents or suicide, but they must realize you're onto them now if they know you went to see Trudy."

"I guess they don't care what I think, but they probably don't want the police crawling all over these incidents." She hunched forward on the table. "Do you think they know you're here? That the CIA, or whoever you're representing, is in the loop?"

"Hard to tell. If someone was watching us at the theater, he spotted us together." His blue eyes narrowed. "She's leaving."

Nicole jerked her head up and watched as Marley took off down the street. "Wherever they're getting together for this wake must be close, because it looks like she's heading in the opposite direction of the station."

"Then we'll have plenty of time to do our search."

When Marley rounded the corner, Slade pushed back from the table. "Let's go."

They crossed the street and let themselves in the front door of the building with Trudy's key. They paused on the stairs and put on the gloves Slade had insisted they bring. A second key worked for the door to the apartment, and Slade clicked it behind them and slid the lock across the top.

When Nicole raised her brows at him, he shrugged. "Better to have Marley trying to figure out how her door got locked from the inside than having her walk in on us tossing her place."

"Let's start with Trudy's bedroom." Nicole made a beeline for the short hallway off the living room and turned into the bedroom on the right-hand side, a stark contrast to the rest of the apartment. "Ah, this is much better."

"Well, we know who the messy one is. It'll be easier to search in here, too."

Nicole took a turn around the neatly ordered room with its stacks of fabric-covered boxes and shelves lined with books and accented with framed photos.

"I'm going to start looking in here." Slade grabbed the knob of the closet door and folded the door back. He held up the stubby key. "A box or safe for this."

Feeling like a voyeur, Nicole eased open the nightstand drawer.

She scanned the contents of the drawer, her gaze tripping over a few condoms, a small bottle of massage oil, some matches and a dog-eared paperback— a pulp fiction Western from the '40s. The title of the book blurred through the tears in her eyes. That book had belonged to Lars.

Sniffling, she picked up the paperback and thumbed through it. Lars had loved the old American West, and it seemed as if Trudy had loved Lars.

She ran a hand across the cover and placed it back in the drawer. "Find anything yet?"

"Nothing. She doesn't have a safe in the closet. You?"

Nicole closed the nightstand drawer. "No."

She wandered to the bookshelves and studied the titles with her head tilted to the side. Lots of plays. Trudy had obviously taken her craft seriously.

Nicole took a seat on the padded stool in front of the vanity, very similar to the one Trudy had been sitting at the night she died. She poked through the makeup and brushes and then hunched forward to study the photos wedged in the mirror's frame.

She caught her breath. "She has a selfie of her and Lars."

Sneezing, Slade backed out of the closet. "Recent?"

She plucked the photo from the mirror. "According to the time stamp, from his last visit here."

"That's strange." Slade hovered over her shoulder at the vanity. "Who prints out selfies? Most people leave them on their phones."

"Trudy obviously had a thing for photographs." She waved at the framed pictures on the shelves.

"Where was it taken?"

"Not sure." She brought the picture to her nose. "Looks like a fast food place or something. See the sign behind them?"

"Hot dogs." Slade poked the picture with his finger. "No, corn dogs. That's an R and an N."

"Corn dogs? I don't know many places in the city that sell corn dogs."

He flicked the picture with his finger. "Who says they're in the city? Look at the sky to the right of the corn dog place. Do you see any other buildings behind them?"

She niggled her bottom lip between her teeth. "Corn dogs. The last time I ate a corn dog was when I took my out-of-town friend and her daughter to Coney Island."

"Could that be Coney Island?"

"Could be, which would help, wouldn't it?" Nicole slipped the photo in her pocket. "It's probably important to figure out every place they went while Lars was here."

"Would help a lot." Slade leaned in closer, his hand brushing her shoulder. "Any more pictures of Lars?"

"Not here—a few group shots on the shelf, all older."

"I don't see much else in here, do you? Let's check out the bathroom."

With shoulders colliding, they crowded the entrance to the small bathroom, where chaos reigned supreme.

Nicole shook her head. "I honestly don't see how

Trudy put up with such a slob. Marley's going to have a hard time finding another roommate."

Slade squeezed past her and tugged open the medicine cabinet. "Do you think this is how Trudy's killers found out about her epilepsy?"

"Maybe." She joined him at the sink and nudged a few prescription bottles with the tip of her finger. "If the police ever do get around to investigating her death as a crime, hopefully they'll find some evidence here."

"In the meantime, we haven't found much except a picture possibly taken at Coney Island. It doesn't look like she kept Lars's film, whatever its form, here in her apartment."

"Unless it's somewhere in that mess." Nicole wedged her hands on her hips and tipped her head toward the living room.

"I don't think Trudy would leave something that important in this jumble of stuff, especially if the stuff belonged to her roommate."

"Probably not. Do you think it would be too obvious to ask Marley if she was here when Lars visited and where Trudy took him?"

"She might think it's weird, but what of it? Marley's not trying to hide anything. Give her another try. You can make up some reason—maybe just trying to figure out what he left you."

"I'll give her a call. Now, let's get out here." She

eyed the creeping shadows in the room and shivered. "I don't like being in someone else's space."

"You'd make a lousy thief." Slade unlocked the inside deadbolt and then closed and locked the door behind them—just as they'd found it.

She trudged down the three flights of stairs ahead of Slade, since the staircase was too narrow for them to walk side by side. She tripped once, clutching the banister.

"Whoa!" He touched her waist. "Careful."

A smile curved her mouth. When Slade Gallagher had your back—literally—it was like having a guardian angel flapping his wings around you. Except Slade's wings were a pair of muscled arms.

They stepped onto the sidewalk as the sky dimmed around them.

"You must be starving, because I am and I had some breakfast. Do you want to pick up Chanel and check on Livvy?"

"Speaking of Livvy, I wonder if the idiots figured out yet that they targeted the wrong person."

"Even if they haven't figured it out, the driver must have realized by now that the accident didn't result in a fatality. He'd be watching the news for sure."

"I must be the only one left standing between them and that film." Nicole pulled off her gloves and shoved them into her purse. "Scary thought."

"Nicole? That you?"

At the sound of Marley's voice behind them, Slade

stiffened beside Nicole and took her arm, squeezing it in warning. He didn't have to warn her. She'd play it cool, even though she felt anything but.

Nicole pasted a smile on her face and turned around, almost tripping over her own feet when she saw a man next to Marley. Good thing her guardian angel still had possession of her arm. "Marley."

"Did you forget something?" Marley stumbled and her own guardian angel grabbed her around the waist.

"No, no." Nicole tilted back her head. "Are we back on your block? We just stayed in the neighborhood and then grabbed a late lunch."

"Well, I drank a late lunch." Marley's laugh ended on a hiccup and a sob.

The man's arm moved to Marley's shoulders. "Sorry, she is a little upset. You understand."

The man's slight accent matched his formal phrasing. "Of course, yes. I'm sorry. I'm Nicole and this is S-Steve."

She'd almost forgotten Slade's made-up name.

"Hello, I'm Conrad."

"Nicole knew Trudy, too. Wasn't she the best, Nicole? Wasn't she the best roommate ever?"

"Yeah, she was." Slade pinched Nicole's arm, and she cleared her throat. "You know, I thought of something after I left your place, Marley. Where did Trudy take Lars when he was visiting?"

"Shh." Marley put two fingers to her lips, smearing her lipstick across her mouth. "Conrad was going out with Trudy."

"Oh." Nicole put up her hands. "Lars was Trudy's friend. She probably mentioned him to you."

"We had just started dating each other, nothing exclusive." Conrad shrugged. "I am going to help Marley home. She drank much in a short time. Please excuse us."

"Take care, Marley."

Marley's head dropped to the side, resting against Conrad's arm. "'Night."

Slade's hand pressed against the small of Nicole's back as he propelled her down the street. "It's a good thing Marley was drunk. She probably won't even remember meeting us in front of her building."

"Probably not, unless Herr Conrad tells her, but like you said, I don't really care if she's suspicious of my motives. I already told her that Trudy was going to give me something from Lars. She can think what she wants. At least Conrad didn't seem too upset about Trudy hanging out with Lars."

"The way he was touching Marley, I think Conrad has already moved on." Slade finally slowed his pace as they rounded the next corner. "I wish we really *had* been eating lunch. I'm hungry."

"I think there's a block of trendy restaurants and bars around here—probably where Marley got her drink on." Nicole pulled out her phone. "I'll look it up."

Fifteen minutes later, they were sitting inside an Italian restaurant with a bottle of red wine between them.

Nicole took a sip from her glass and closed her eyes as the warmth from the wine spread through her chest. "I'm going to give Livvy a call. Maybe the police found out something about the car that hit her."

"Try to get some info on the car or driver." Slade held up a piece of buttery garlic bread from the basket the waiter had just dropped at the table. "Don't mind me. I'm going to devour this."

Rolling her eyes, Nicole placed the call to Livvy.

"Hi, Nicole. I'm still alive."

"Don't even joke about it. What's the verdict?"

"Broken foot. How's that for a dog walker?"

"I'm so sorry. For a little extra money, do you and Andi want to keep Chanel there? I'm sure my mom would be fine with it, and I'm…" She glanced at Slade wolfing down his second piece of garlic bread. "Kind of busy."

"That would be great, if you're sure Mimi won't mind."

"Believe me, my mom trusts you with Chanel much more than she does me. Send Andi over to pick up Chanel's food and toys, and I'll have a check for you."

"Thanks, Nicole."

Between bites, Slade nudged the toe of her shoe with his own.

"Livvy, did you remember anything more about the car or the driver?"

"Just a dark blur, and I didn't see the driver at all."

"Did anyone else? Were there any witnesses?"

"One guy said he saw the car speed up coming around the corner, but he didn't get a make or model. Said it was a man driving, though." She coughed. "I told the cops all this."

"I'm just curious. Have Andi come by tomorrow for Chanel's stuff and tell her to give me a call first."

"Will do. Thanks for checking on me."

Nicole ended the call and took another sip of wine—she needed it. "Hit-and-run, no witnesses."

"Not surprising." Slade shoved the bread basket her way. "Have some before I inhale the rest."

She picked up a piece of garlic bread and ripped it in half. "If they were trying to kill me by running me over, they must not be interested in recovering the footage."

"Maybe they already know what's on it and just want to stop anyone else from seeing it."

"How do they know Lars didn't copy and send the footage to multiple people?"

"They don't." Slade wiped his greasy fingers on a napkin and then swirled his wine before taking a sip. "But whatever outcome they fear from having that film go public or having it fall into the hands of the wrong people obviously hasn't occurred yet.

They know nobody has made any significant sense of what Lars filmed—including Lars."

"So it can't just be the interview subjects speaking out on behalf of women's rights. If that were the case, they'd want that film so they could punish those women." She slumped in her chair and stuffed some bread in her mouth. "I don't get it."

"Give your brain a rest and eat." Slade gestured to the waiter, who came scurrying back to their table.

They both ordered the lasagna and a salad to share, and Nicole hadn't realized how hungry she was until later when she dug into the food.

As she twined her fork around a strand of cheese, she said, "I'm going to have to come back here. The food's great."

"Maybe it's just your hunger that makes it seem special."

Or maybe it was the company. She dabbed some tomato sauce from the corner of her mouth. "You've practically licked your plate, and you're trying to tell me you didn't enjoy it?"

"I didn't say I didn't like it." He pressed his thumb against her chin. "I liked everything about this meal."

Her cheeks flushed. "Do I have marinara sauce all over my face?"

"No."

She parted her lips on a quick breath, waiting for his explanation of why he'd touched her chin.

His crooked smile told her he didn't plan to give her one. "More wine?"

"Two glasses with food is my limit. No food, one glass."

"And what's your limit for some faceless stalker out gunning for you? I think you have a good excuse to imbibe."

"Since he's still out there gunning for me, I should've limited myself to water. In fact, I'm going to have a cappuccino."

"I guess Marley doesn't have the same rules as you do. Maybe you can hit her up tomorrow when she's sober and ask her if she knows where Trudy and Lars went."

"I'd better give her plenty of time to get past her hangover, and we may have already nailed down one place, if that corn dog stand matches up to the one in Coney Island."

"We can check it out when we get back to your place tonight, but if they did go there, it's probably significant. Who goes to an amusement park when you feel your life is in danger?" Slade pushed away his own half-full wineglass. "You know what? I'm gonna miss Chanel."

Nicole snorted. "Liar."

"I'm totally serious." His eyebrows formed a V over his nose. "I've always had dogs, but my current lifestyle doesn't allow pets."

"Your current lifestyle doesn't allow a lot of

things. Wife?" She held her breath. She couldn't believe she hadn't asked him this question before. What if she'd been salivating over another woman's husband?

"No wife, but some guys manage. We do go home between deployments."

She thanked the waiter for her coffee and picked up the thread of the conversation. "Must be tough on their wives."

"The ones I know are some of the strongest women I've ever met. They make it possible for those guys to do their jobs."

His blue eyes kindled with admiration. Slade Gallagher seemed to appreciate strong women.

Her phone buzzed in her pocket, and she pulled it out. "It's Marley. Maybe she thought of something. Hi, Marley."

A man responded in accented English. "Sorry, this is not Marley. I met you when I walked her home."

"Conrad, right?"

Slade glanced up from studying the check.

"That is correct."

"Is Marley okay?"

"She is fine, just...snockered." He paused for a few seconds. "I think I know what Trudy's friend Lars left for you."

"You do?" She kicked Slade under the table and turned on her phone's speaker, keeping the volume low.

"Yes, I have something and can give it to you to-night, if you like."

Slade hunched forward, his head cocked toward the phone on the table between them.

"What is it?"

"It is in a padded envelope. Do you want me to open it?"

"No, please. I'll come and get it. You're still at Marley's?" He had to be if he was using her cell phone.

"I left her sleeping and do not want to disturb her, but I'm still in the area. Are you still in Brooklyn, or did you go back to Manhattan?"

"I—I'm still here. We decided to have dinner before going home." She frowned at Slade. "Why do you still have her phone if you left her place?"

"I am returning to her place. You understand."

"Completely." She smirked at Slade. He'd been right about Conrad moving on from Trudy. "I can meet you."

"That is perfect. I'm at a bar on Union, and there is a small park across the street. Can we meet there?"

Slade tapped her hand and lifted his shoulders with his hands out.

She nodded. "Why there and not the bar?"

"Trudy told me something about this package. I want to give it to you in private."

"Okay. What time?"

"Thirty minutes by the playground on the corner of the park."

As soon as she ended the call, Slade said, "That was strange. Why would Trudy give the package to him?"

"Maybe she didn't. Maybe she told him about it, and when he met me tonight he decided to get it from her place and hand it over to me."

"You should've told him I was coming along."

"I'm sure he knows that." She tapped the check on the table. "Let's take care of this and get over there. I'll have just enough time to finish my cappuccino. Maybe this is our lucky night."

"I don't trust the guy. Why wouldn't he just meet us in the bar?"

"Remember Dave? He didn't want to be seen with us, either."

"Yeah, but Dave had already talked to Lars. This guy Conrad probably never met Lars and doesn't have a clue about what's going on, and how did he know you live in Manhattan?"

"Marley could've mentioned it. Besides, he was dating Trudy. She probably told him about Lars's strange request. Conrad ran into me tonight and figured he'd hand over the package."

"Or maybe once he put a *snockered* Marley to bed, he thought he'd try his luck with you."

"And he just happens to know about Lars and the

package?" She rolled her eyes. "This is our chance, Slade. Let's take it."

"All right, but I'll be right by your side."

"I'm counting on it." In fact, she wouldn't have it any other way.

Twenty minutes later, they strolled up to the park with the empty playground on the corner.

Slade faced the well-lit bar across the street. "I feel like marching in there and telling him to hand over the package. This is ridiculous."

"And scare him off?" She shoved her hands in the pockets of her jacket and kicked at some bark in the playground. "Let's just wait for him."

The chains on the swings creaked in the wind, and Nicole hugged her jacket around her. She'd rather be in that bar than out here, too.

Slade started whistling, and she turned toward him to ask the name of the song. She jerked back, her eyes widening. "What is that red light on your forehead?"

"Red light on my...get down!"

Then her easygoing SEAL lost all his senses as he lunged at her and tackled her to the ground.

Chapter Eight

Slade heard the bullet whiz over his head as he took Nicole down.

Her knee gouged his thigh as he landed on top of her, and she grunted softly. He'd probably knocked the wind out of her.

His lips close to her ear, he whispered, "Stay down. That red light you saw on my forehead was a laser marking the spot for a bullet."

She gasped beneath him and then choked. "Where did it come from? Are they still out there?"

"Let's get over to the slide, but stay down." He'd pulled his weapon from his pocket and clutched it in his hand, finger on the trigger.

Nicole must've done this before because she assumed the position and army crawled through the bark to the base of the slide.

Slade stayed behind her, his gaze scanning the tops of the trees. When they reached the slide, he rolled over and studied the skyline. He nudged Nicole's shoulder and pointed to a three-story building next to the bar. "I think he's up there. To get that bead on my forehead, he had to have some height. Unless he's in the trees."

Nicole twisted her head over her shoulder to take in the trees behind him. "I'd feel more comfortable knowing where he was before I make a move."

"We don't have to make a move yet. It'll be interesting to see if Gunther shows up."

"It's Conrad, and if you're thinking what I'm thinking, he's not going to make an appearance."

A scuffle of leaves had Slade grabbing Nicole's calf and squeezing. "Shh."

The wind picked up his hushed whisper and rustled the branches of the trees with it. If Conrad wasn't the shooter, he could be on his way to deflect suspicion—or to make sure his man had hit the intended targets.

As they huddled together against the cold plastic of the slide, Nicole's breath came out in short spurts, tickling the back of his neck.

His muscles ached with the tension, and his eyes burned in their sockets as he peered into the darkness, his gaze darting from the swings stirring in the breeze to the shadows cast by the jungle gym.

He eased out one long breath between clenched teeth.

"We're going to get out of here—on our bellies. I don't want you standing up until we reach the sidewalk, and you're staying on my left. We don't want to give this sniper any opportunity."

"Got it. Wouldn't want to make it easy for him."

"Head down, face in the bark, let's move."

A split second later, Nicole flattened her body against the scattered pieces of bark and scooted out from their hiding place. He kept to her left from where he figured the first shot had been fired. He hoped it was the last shot.

He sealed his lips against the dry bark as it scratched his chin and the side of his jaw. They couldn't give the shooter one glimpse of their faces, which would give him his bull's-eye. The sniper's scope probably had night vision, but Slade knew too well the difficulty of hitting a dark target level with the ground.

He bumped Nicole's shoulder. "You're doing great, just a few more feet until the sidewalk. We're rolling into the gutter and hunching behind that car."

"Can't wait."

Slade's hands skimmed the rough cement of the sidewalk as he extended his body into a human log and launched himself at the gutter.

Nicole hit first with a thud.

"Are you okay?"

"I rolled faster than I thought I would. I guess that happens when you're fueled with fear and cappuccino."

Slade grabbed the bumper of the car and pulled

himself up to his knees. He put an arm around Nicole's shoulders as she crouched beside him. "We're going to cross the street, hover in that doorway and wait for the next taxi. Are you ready?"

"What I'd like to do is go into that bar and find Conrad."

"Not a great idea."

"Do you think he's in there waiting for some kind of signal?"

"I could give him a signal…or two, but I doubt he's in the bar, and we don't need to expose ourselves any more tonight." He grabbed her hand and they ran across the street, doubled over at the waist.

A taxi came out of nowhere and honked at them, and Slade pounded on the hood to stop it since they might not find another.

The driver's scowl melted away when he realized they wanted a ride. He took them to the train station, and ten minutes later they collapsed into a couple of seats as the train lurched into motion.

Nicole's eyelashes dropped for about a minute and then she was studying him with that curious spark in her green eyes. "Conrad hit up Trudy after she met with Lars, probably fished for info about Lars and then killed her when he found out we were in contact with her. Does that about sum it up?"

"I don't think she was killed just because we contacted her, and you forgot the part where he tried to have us killed, too."

She smacked her forehead with the heel of her hand. "Silly me."

He gave voice to one more concern. "I hope Trudy's roommate is going to be safe."

"Oh, God." Nicole plowed her hands through her hair, loosening stray bits of bark. "I'd call her, but Conrad has her phone."

Slade dragged his own phone from his jacket pocket. "I can place an anonymous call to the police to do a well check at Marley's place. I can say we saw a man carrying her into the building, which is pretty close to the truth. At least that might get the police over there and scare off Conrad if he has any plans of returning."

"Could you do that? I'd feel better and not like we completely abandoned her."

"We can't check on Marley ourselves. We could be walking right into an ambush." He held up the phone. "I'll make the call."

Nicole listened intently as he spoke to the police and grabbed his arm when he ended the call. "What was that all about?"

"Seems we got a little lucky, if you want to call it that. There may be a serial rapist in the area, and the police are going to check it out right away."

"That's terrible, even though it's a win for Marley. Could this night get any worse?"

A muscle jumped in Slade's jaw as he turned his head to the side. "I think it just did."

YOUR FAVORITE SUSPENSE NOVELS!

GET 2 FREE BOOKS!

2 FREE BOOKS

To get your 2 free books, affix this peel-off sticker to the reply card and mail it today!

Plus, receive

TWO FREE BONUS GIFTS!

We'd like to send you two free books from the series you are enjoying now. Your two books have a combined cover price of over $10 retail, but are yours to keep absolutely FREE! We'll even send you two wonderful surprise gifts. You can't lose!

Each of your FREE books features unique characters, interesting settings and captivating stories you won't want to miss!

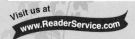

GET 2 FREE BOOKS!

CLAIM NOW!
Return this card today to get 2 FREE Books and 2 FREE Bonus Gifts!

YES! Please send me the **2 FREE books** and **2 FREE bonus gifts** for which I qualify. I understand that I am under no obligation to purchase anything further, as explained on the back of this card.

PLACE FREE GIFTS SEAL HERE

❏ I prefer the regular-print edition
182/382 HDL GLUQ

❏ I prefer the larger-print edition
199/399 HDL GLUQ

FIRST NAME

LAST NAME

ADDRESS

APT.#

CITY

STATE/PROV.

ZIP/POSTAL CODE

◀ **DETACH AND MAIL CARD TODAY!** ▶

® and ™ are trademarks owned and used by the trademark owner and/or its licensee.
© 2016 HARLEQUIN ENTERPRISES LIMITED. Printed in the U.S.A.

HI-517-FMIVY17

Her knee bumped his as she jerked her head in his direction. She squinted into the glass partition to the next car. "What do you see?"

"A man moving down the center aisle in the next car. He's hunching forward like he doesn't want to be seen."

"Then he's successful, because I don't see anything except a woman reading and a man with big headphones on."

Slade sat up straighter, craning his neck and lifting his chin. "I swear I saw him. He must be slouched in a seat."

Nicole slouched herself, sticking her legs in front of her. "I don't want to see him, either. I'm exhausted."

Licking his lips, Slade glanced to his left, where a couple had their heads together over a cell phone, looking at pictures. Beyond them, a single man and two young women took up a few seats between them and the next car.

"I think we should move." Slade lurched to his feet and grabbed her hand.

"If he comes after us, we're going to run out of train."

"Not if we move fast enough. We'll get to the station in Manhattan before he gets to us."

She tilted her head to the side to look past his body into the next car. "I still don't…"

Her words died on her lips as a head with a dark

cap popped up and back down. She gasped. "Did you see that?"

"I did. I'm thinking we were followed. Get moving to the next car and stay in front of me."

The man in their car glanced at them with half-hearted interest as they shuffled down the length of the train car.

When they reached the end of the car, Slade gave the door a shove and they stumbled into the next car. This one contained a few more people than the previous one, but nobody seemed to care about a couple bursting into their space.

Slade twisted his head over his shoulder and said, "He's on the move."

Nicole stumbled as she reached for a seatback to steady herself. The train curved to the right and the rails squealed.

"Keep going." Slade propelled her forward with a hand on the small of her back.

Nicole was panting now and slammed two hands against the next connecting door. It burst open.

The faces in the next car stood out sharply as Slade's gaze darted from person to person. He just wanted to put as much space as possible between Nicole and the impending doom tracking them through the train.

Of course, that guy would have to get through him to get to her, and he'd never allow that.

As they crashed into the next car, Nicole said, "Only one more car before we're trapped."

"He'll be trapped, too. I just don't want things to get messy on the train."

"Messy?" Her eyes widened as her gaze dropped to the bulge of his hand in his pocket. He wouldn't hesitate to use his weapon in this public place to protect her—after all, that's what he did. The guy following them through the train wouldn't hesitate to use his, either.

They hustled into the last car just as an announcement came over the loudspeaker that the next stop was in Manhattan.

Nicole turned and lined up her spine against a silver pole, wedging her feet against the floor of the car. She could slide down that thing in a second if she had to. Would the attacker come in with guns blazing?

Slade made a half turn and squeezed Nicole's arm. "Get ready to hit the deck."

Nodding, she squared her shoulders and tensed her body. He knew he could count on her to follow his direction.

As he started to move back toward the previous car, she grabbed on to his belt loop. "You're going the wrong way, aren't you?"

"I'm going to be his welcoming committee." Slade reached the door connecting the last car to the previous one and hopped onto the seat to the left of it.

This action finally got the attention of the handful of people in the car.

Slade raised his voice. "There's a man with a gun. Everybody get down."

Not everyone in the car listened, so Nicole nudged the leg of the woman sitting across from her. "He's serious."

Another woman screamed, and as the train slowed to a stop, their pursuer shoved open the final set of doors.

But Slade was ready for him.

Chapter Nine

The man raised his weapon. Slade swung from the bars. He hit the guy dead center with both feet. The man flew backward, his gun spinning from his hand. He crashed against some empty seats.

People in both cars tumbled out of the train onto the platform, a shrill voice raised, calling for the police.

The man sprawled half on the seat, his knees on the floor, but it didn't stop him from reaching for his weapon. Slade got there first, stomping on the man's wrist with his foot.

He snatched up the gun and then got in the man's pale face and growled, "If this wasn't a public place, you'd be dead. Next time."

Slade slipped back into the last car where Nicole was still waiting for him. He took her arm just as two police officers boarded the train.

"Did you see a man with a gun?"

"I didn't see a gun, but there was a fight back

there." Slade jerked his thumb over his shoulder and guided Nicole from the car before any more questions could come up.

Once they got onto the platform, they both picked up the pace, maneuvering through the crowds.

"Is he…was he…"

"The bastard's still alive. I can't leave a dead man in the middle of a train, but I have his weapon and maybe we can get some prints. He wasn't wearing gloves."

"Will the police arrest him?"

"On what charge? He has no gun, unless he has a spare on him, and he'll just claim someone attacked him on the train and will refuse to pursue the matter. The other side has even less reason to get mixed up with local law enforcement than I do."

When they got to street level, Nicole grabbed on to a lamppost, her body sagging against it.

Slade curled an arm around her waist, and her slight frame trembled against him. "I'm sorry, Nicole. We need to get out of here. I don't know how badly I hurt him. He could come after us again."

She blinked her eyes a few times and tossed her hair over her shoulder. "I know. I'm okay. I'll snag us a taxi."

And she did just that. He expected her to collapse in the backseat, lean against him, but she pinned her shoulders against the seat of the taxi and cleared her throat.

"They're going to take any opportunity they can to kill me, aren't they?"

"Looks like they don't want you getting your hands on the film—whether or not you know what to do with it."

"They have to figure my current companion—" she jabbed his arm with her index finger "—is more than some guy on the street. That has to have them doubly desperate."

"I guess Trudy never did tell Conrad what Lars gave her. He doesn't know what he's looking for."

"But we do."

She outlined the bulge in the pocket of his jeans and for a quick minute he thought she was making a move on him, but she was just tracing the outline of Trudy's key chain. "And as soon as I get home and back to my computer, I'm going to do a little research on the lockers at Coney Island."

Slade patted his jacket pocket. "And I'm going to find out where I need to take this gun to get fingerprinted. Maybe we can narrow down the group that's after this film if we can start ID'ing some of its members. We have Conrad, the owner of this gun and the sniper who was taking potshots at us."

"Potshots? That seemed like more than a potshot to me."

He snorted. "Amateur."

"So, we could be dealing with three different people here in New York, or maybe someone's doing double duty."

"I don't believe Conrad was the sniper. Conrad had to be available in case we sauntered into that bar instead of meeting him at the park. They could've even used him to track us down in the park so the sniper could get off his shots."

"Do you think the man chasing us through the train was the sniper?"

"No. He got after us too quickly. That sniper was probably still in position waiting for another opportunity when we jumped into the taxi. So, yeah, we could be looking at three different people."

"They're sparing no expense or manpower—whoever *they* are." She wrapped her arms around her lithe body and shivered. "If you hadn't shown up when you did, I'd be a goner by now. There's no way I would've known how to handle this onslaught."

"I don't know." He smoothed his hand down her arm. "You're pretty savvy in the field. It's clear you've had practice at this."

"I've been in some gnarly situations, but these people just keep coming at me from all directions." She covered her eyes with one hand. "I'm not sure how much more I can handle."

"You don't have to handle it alone, Nicole." He patted her knee. "I'm right here."

The taxi squealed to a stop in front of her mother's

building. She shoved some crumpled bills at the driver in the front seat and said, "Time to get to work."

Slade's senses were on high alert from the curb to the elevator, but once inside the car, he wedged a shoulder against the mirrored wall and released a long breath. Back to work.

Toby, the nighttime doorman, had assured them on the way in that nothing unusual had happened at the building and no strangers had been sniffing around. But Slade still approached Nicole's apartment as if he expected to find armed assailants hiding behind the drapes. He flicked back the drapes with the barrel of his gun under Nicole's watchful eye.

"Are you going to check out the entire place before we get down to business?"

"Just a quick surveillance. Any more news from Livvy?"

"Just a text that Chanel is doing fine."

"Nothing from Marley, I suppose…or Conrad?"

"He's probably trashed the phone by now. He won't be going back to Marley now that we're onto him, but we need to find a way to contact her to warn her about Conrad."

"We'll get to her. Don't worry."

He searched the place more carefully than he'd let on to Nicole, and only then did he unclench his jaw and relax his muscles.

He must've communicated his tension to her, because she hadn't moved from her post by the corner of the kitchen, arms and legs crossed, since he started his survey.

He nodded to her. "All clear. Do you wanna break out the computer?"

"I wanna break out a bottle of wine. You up for that?"

"Absolutely. I'm glad you changed your mind because we deserve it." He cocked his head at her as she pulled that bottle of white from the fridge. "You know, I don't think I ever thanked you for saving my life tonight."

"I saved your life?" She twisted the cork out of the bottle with a small pop. "All I remember is you swinging through the train car like Tarzan."

"At the park. You saw that red dot on my forehead."

"Yeah, I was such an idiot, it didn't occur to me what that was." She poured the golden liquid into two glasses and then tipped a little more into each.

"You noticed it, which is more than most people would." He took the glass from her hand, the tips of his fingers brushing across her knuckles. Her skin felt smooth and soft and ignited a longing in his chest that he hadn't felt in years.

Her lips parted, and her lashes dipped once as if in acknowledgment of his silent yearning. Then she flashed her pearly whites and gulped back some wine, breaking the spell.

"Then you're welcome, but I owed you big-time for taking down that pirate. A small token of my gratitude."

He took a swig of the expensive sauvignon blanc, the fruity taste flaring in his mouth before he swallowed. "Why'd you spit on him?"

"What?"

"The pirate. I watched you through my scope after I took him down, and you spit on his body."

"Did I?" Her laugh gurgled in the back of her throat. "What a barbarian I am. I suppose it was instinct. I was so mad that we'd been captured. So terrified. So relieved. When that many emotions are running through your mind all at the same time, I guess your animal instincts take over. You must've thought I was a crazy woman."

"I thought it was pretty kick-ass."

A small smile curved her lips. "We still have some work to do. Where are you taking that gun?"

"I'm going to send an email from my phone right now." He pointed across the great room. "Office?"

"Yeah." She wrapped her fingers around the neck of the wine bottle. "I'm taking this along."

As he followed her into the office, he said, "I miss Chanel. It's too quiet around here without her."

"That little puff of fur turned into a real hero, didn't she? She practically saved Livvy."

"That was when the people after you were still trying to make their hits look like accidents. The sniper tonight and the guy on the train indicate a level of frustration that just turned dangerous."

She sat down in front of the computer and woke it up with a flick of the mouse. "I think Giles, Lars and Trudy already found it dangerous—lethal, in fact."

"Of course. That's not what I meant." He brought up the secure email on his phone and sent a message to Ariel about the gun he'd taken from the man on the train.

Nicole had been busy clicking away on her computer and now leaned back in her chair. "This is interesting."

He crossed to the desk in two long strides and ducked his head over Nicole's shoulder to peer at the monitor with its display of colorful pictures. "What's this?"

"It's Coney Island, home of corn dog stands."

"Did you find the place that was in Trudy's picture?"

"Not yet, but look at this."

He leaned in closer, and despite diving into the dirt at the playground and rolling around the floor of a train, Nicole still smelled like fresh flowers.

She tapped the screen at his hesitation. "Lockers. Coney Island has lockers, the type you originally had pegged for Trudy's key."

"Good sleuthing. Seems pretty risky for Lars to leave something as important as that film in an amusement park locker, though."

"Risky but unexpected. Anyone might guess a safe-deposit box or safe under the bed, but a locker at the beach?" She raised her arms over her head in a stretch, interlocking her fingers. "I can't think of anywhere else close where that picture could've been taken. Of course, they could've gone to other places while Lars was out here and just didn't take any pics."

"Yeah, but Lars's visit wasn't a vacation. He came through New York specifically to hand off the film to you and in your absence gave it to Trudy instead. I doubt Trudy took him to all the tourist spots."

"It's too bad I wasn't here."

"I don't know about that. I wasn't here, either, and you didn't have the same level of suspicion then. You would've been an easy target." His hands moved to her shoulders in a protective move.

"I'm glad you're here." She tapped his knuckles with her fingertips.

His hold on her shoulders turned into a caress, and she seemed to melt beneath his touch. Dropping to his knees next to her chair, he wedged a finger beneath her chin and turned her head toward him.

He ran the pad of his thumb across her bottom lip, waiting for some sign that this wasn't the stupidest idea on the planet.

She sighed, her breath tickling his thumb, and her eyelashes fluttered.

He took that as two signs. Angling his mouth over

hers, he touched his lips to her lips. The wine he'd just consumed tasted better this way.

Nicole closed her eyes and twined her arms around his neck, pulling him into her special realm where everything seemed more intense—the taste of the wine, her sweet scent, the pillowy softness of her lips, the music of her sighs.

He deepened the kiss, his tongue probing for hers, toying with it in a sensuous dance that ignited a flame in his belly. The thudding of his heart drowned out the voices in his head that had been urging caution from the minute he'd laid eyes on this woman through his scope.

With her arms still coiled around his neck and her lips pressed against his, he slid one hand down her back and the other beneath her thighs and pulled her into his arms. From his knees, he rose to his feet with a tight hold on this long-limbed beauty.

He didn't even have any idea where her bedroom was in the vast area upstairs, but he'd be happy to take her anywhere.

Slade moved from the office with the precious bundle in his arms and made for the stairs.

Nicole had broken their kiss when he'd lifted her from the chair in the office. Now she cupped his face in her hands. "You do not have to carry me upstairs."

Looking into her green eyes, he narrowed his gaze. "Because you don't want this?"

"Oh, I want whatever this is, but you don't have to lug me up the staircase to get it."

He chuckled. Yep, like no other high-maintenance society girl he'd ever met.

"No lugging required. You're as light as a feather."

"That may be, but I just survived a sniper's bullet and an attack on the train. I'm not going to risk tumbling down the stairs, even if I do end up on top of a hot Navy SEAL."

"You don't have to take a fall down the stairs to wind up on top of this Navy SEAL."

He winked at her as he set her down on the bottom step of the winding staircase.

Just as she took his hand and he felt like his head might explode, the jangling ring of a telephone jarred his senses.

"What the hell is that?"

"It's called a telephone. It's my mom's landline, which she refuses to give up."

"It's gotta be close to midnight. Who's calling her at this hour?" Even as he asked the question, a whisper of apprehension made the hair on the back of his neck stand at attention.

"The phone has an answering machine, so whoever it is can leave a message." She tugged on his shirtsleeve.

As he planted a foot on the next step, the person on the other end of the phone did start leaving a message—one they could hear.

A man's accented voice rushed over the line. "Nicole. It's Dahir. We need to talk. It's urgent—life or death."

Chapter Ten

She jerked away from the promise of Slade's warm touch and stumbled off the bottom step. She pounced on the phone in the kitchen, Dahir's voice acting like a magnet.

"Dahir? Dahir? It's Nicole."

Her translator grunted in surprise. "Nicole? You're there? I didn't know you'd be at this number."

She could've asked him why he'd called her mother's place, but he was probably just hitting up all her numbers. "Well, I am here, and I'm so happy to hear from you. You're well? Safe?"

"I am. I am. You heard about the others? Giles? Lars?"

Slade touched her arm, and she punched a button to put the phone on speaker. "Of course I heard. Giles's death was a tragedy, but when Lars supposedly committed suicide, I knew something wasn't right. Where are you?"

"I'm here in New York. That's why I cannot believe in my…luck that you are here, too."

"How did you get here? I've been trying to track you down forever."

"After the kidnapping, I had to hide out. It wasn't safe for me—or my family."

"I'm so sorry, but how did you manage to get to New York? Did the US government help you after all?" She glanced at Slade, hunched over the counter, but he shrugged.

"I can't really say, Nicole. I'm here now, and I must meet with you."

"Do you know why Giles and Lars were killed?"

Slade tugged on a lock of her hair and put a finger over his lips.

She drew her brows over her nose. He didn't trust Dahir?

"I have a good idea why they were killed. That's why I need to talk to you."

Slade tapped the telephone receiver.

"Can you just tell me now over the phone?"

"I can't, Nicole. I have to give you something in person."

Her heart jumped. "Lars's film? Do you have Lars's footage of the interviews we did with the women?"

"I can't tell you over the phone. It has to be in person. I'll tell you everything tomorrow night."

"Tomorrow night? Why not earlier? I'll meet you anywhere."

"I can't make it until nighttime. There are…things

I need to do first, and please don't talk to anyone else about this or do anything else to find the film. It's not what you think."

Dahir's voice had gotten louder, his accent thicker.

"Are you okay, Dahir?"

"I'm fine." His voice cracked. "It's my family who's in danger. Please just do as I ask you."

"I will. I will."

Slade nudged her foot with the toe of his shoe and she waved him off.

"I'm staying with a friend in Harlem. There's a club not far from his place. It's dark, crowded, noisy. We'll meet there."

He gave her the name of the club and told her to be there at eleven o'clock.

"Nicole?"

"Yes."

"Come by yourself."

"I'll see you then, Dahir. Be careful."

"You, too."

When she ended the call, Slade exploded. "You are *not* meeting that guy at eleven o'clock at night in some club by yourself."

"It's Dahir. I trust him."

"Trust nobody, and even if he's on the up-and-up, how do you know he hasn't been followed? He might lead whoever killed Giles, Lars and Trudy right to you."

"I think it's a chance we have to take. Maybe he has the film. Maybe Lars left a copy with him."

"I'm coming with you." He held up his hands as she opened her mouth. "I'll stay out of sight, but if you think I'm letting you walk into some lion's den by yourself, you're smoking something."

"I'm not smoking anything, and I'm counting on your being there. In fact, I'm not making a move without you, but I think we should put our trip to Coney Island tomorrow on hold."

"Why should we?"

"You heard Dahir."

Slade rolled his eyes. "I heard a bunch of gibberish that didn't make much sense."

"He said it's not what I think and warned me against taking any more steps to find the film. His family's lives may depend on that, and I'm not going to be responsible for anyone else getting hurt." She drummed her fingers on the counter. "You know what? The amusement park at Coney Island isn't even open tomorrow, anyway. It's Friday, and until the summer, Luna Park is open on the weekends only so we have to wait."

"Well, that's that, I guess. Okay, we'll see what Dahir has. He may just want help from you. Maybe he's here illegally, because I sure as hell know we didn't bring him over."

"I'll give him that help if that's what it is. Dahir

put his life on the line for us every time he translated for those women and told their stories for them."

"All right. I'll probably get an email back regarding the gun and where to take it for fingerprinting. I can work on that tomorrow while we wait for this meeting. I'm also going to head over to that club and scope it out beforehand."

She stifled a yawn. The moment between them had passed. She didn't know what she was thinking, anyway. She'd been carried away by the gentleness of his touch. She couldn't get involved with another adventurer, no matter how good his kisses felt.

"I, uh, left the wine in the office. I'm going to grab that and put it away…unless you want more."

He watched her beneath heavy-lidded eyes, the tension of his previous expectations melting from his face. "I don't need any more…wine. Are you turning in for the night?"

"I am, Slade. I'm just so tired. It all hit me after Dahir's call. I'm sorry…"

He put two fingers to her lips. "Don't apologize. I'll get the wine and put it away. You get some sleep."

She replaced the phone in its cradle and turned, pausing on a half step. She could have him in her bed, making love to her, holding her. And then what? When this was all over, regardless of the outcome, he'd be halfway across the world protecting someone else, putting his life on the line for someone else—and she'd be waiting for a call. She couldn't lose anyone else, and Slade Gallagher already meant more to her than he should.

Huffing out a breath, she turned toward the staircase. "Good night, Slade."

"Good night, Nicole."

THE NEXT MORNING, Slade beat her to the punch again and did a good job filling her mother's kitchen with his shirtless presence as he made coffee.

Was he trying to make her regret her decision last night? As the muscles in his back bunched and flexed while he reached for the coffee mugs, she wiped a little drool from the corner of her mouth and regretted it mightily.

He swung around, the fingers of one hand hooked in the handles of both mugs, looking like some hunky maid service. "Coffee?"

"Yes, please." She sat at the granite island and sank her chin into the palm of her hand. "You look… chipper."

She'd expected him to be morose and sullen over his missed opportunity last night—just as she was.

"I slept well, despite missing Chanel, and woke up to an encouraging email."

"About the gun?"

"Yeah, I'm supposed to bring it to the FBI office here in Manhattan."

"Am I allowed to tag along?" She pointed to

the fridge as he placed her coffee in front of her. "Soy, please."

"Yeah, of course. I want you tagging along. It's just safer, for now."

"I'm hoping Dahir will hand over the footage tonight. Once you guys have it and turn it over to the CIA, I should be out of the loop, right? There's no reason for this terrorist cell to target me anymore, unless they go in for revenge." She bit her lip as she swirled a stream of soy milk into her coffee. "They're not in that business, are they?"

"We don't exactly know who *they* are. It may not even be a terrorist group." He drummed his fingers on the counter. "That's why it's important to get the prints from this gun today."

"Are they expecting you?"

"In a few hours."

"I'm going to call and check on Livvy before we get going. Did you see anything in the news about an altercation on the train last night?"

"No, but then that wasn't big enough to make it to the local morning news. I'm sure our friend didn't give the NYPD much information."

"I'll take a shower and get dressed. I suppose we'll have to stop off at your hotel again so you can get a change of clothes." She grabbed her coffee mug and slid from the bar stool. "You know, if you're going to make a habit of spending the night here, you might as well just pack a bag."

He opened his mouth to respond, but she twirled around and headed for the stairs. Was she sending him mixed messages? She usually didn't play coy. If she wanted a man, she let him know in no uncertain terms—and she wanted Slade Gallagher.

Forty minutes later she came back downstairs wearing a long cotton skirt and a denim jacket. A visit to the FBI office should be nice and sedate. At least, she wasn't planning on crawling through a playground on her belly or dashing through a moving train. Although with Slade by her side, either one of those was a distinct possibility.

Still parked in the kitchen, Slade glanced up from his phone as she wedged her hip against the center island. "Are we still on schedule for taking in the gun?"

"An Agent Mills is going to meet us."

"How much does he know about our…your assignment?"

His mouth quirked. "Just enough to run the prints through the Department of Justice and Interpol databases, if necessary."

"I hope identifying this guy sheds some light on the motivation behind getting this footage."

"Yeah, I'm beginning to believe more and more that your kidnapping by those pirates is also linked to all of this. That was their first attempt at stopping this film from getting anywhere, but those Somali pirates were freelancers and had their own ideas about what they wanted from your capture."

"Then the SEALs probably saved this group the inconvenience of taking out the pirates themselves."

"Possibly." He'd eaten some eggs for breakfast and put his dishes in the sink.

"You can leave those. Jenny will be over today to clean the place." She felt a warm tinge in her cheeks at the way Slade's mouth tightened. "Honestly, Jenny likes to have something to do when she comes over."

He ran the water in the sink over the dishes. "I'm not judging."

"You kind of had that—" she stretched her lips into a straight line "—disgusted look."

"I'm sorry. It just sort of reminded me of…things."

"I know. I know. High-society, high-maintenance divas." She waved her hands in the air. "Would it make you feel better if I told you my mom was a Vegas showgirl when she met Dad?"

"Really?" His eyebrows jumped to his hairline.

"She was, so while she definitely enjoys the money Dad left her, she never forgets where she came from and our housekeeper, Jenny, adores her. The two of them spend more time gossiping about celebrities than in any kind of lady of the manor–maidservant relationship."

"Is that why your mother is so accepting of what you do and the men you date?"

Nicole snorted. "Accepting, maybe, but she thinks

I'm crazy. She worked long, hard hours as a young woman and doesn't understand why anyone would want to work if they didn't have to. And the men I date? What do you know about them?"

"Not much." He lifted his shoulders. "I know about the guy who died on Everest—sorry."

"Yeah, crazy son of a bitch." She rubbed the end of her tingling nose. "Are you ready?"

"Let's do it."

They took a taxi to Slade's hotel and she tried to wait in the hotel lobby again, but Slade wouldn't hear of it. "Let's just be on the safe side. I won't be long."

This time he spared her the visuals of his perfect body, although she could still hear the shower over the TV and her imagination probably got her hotter than the real thing.

Then he burst from the bathroom in a T-shirt and jeans and she shook her head. Nothing about Slade was hotter than the real thing.

"You okay out here?"

"Just fine." She sat up straighter in the chair and lowered the volume of the TV. "I did take a sparkling water from the minibar, if that's okay. I'll pay you for it."

"I'll itemize it on my expense report." He pulled a plaid shirt over his T-shirt. "I don't think I need a jacket today."

"That's why I'm wearing this." She swished her skirt around her knees. "I think spring is on the way."

He pulled on his boots and stamped his feet. "Okay, let's find out who was chasing us last night."

Handling the weapon carefully, he placed it inside a manila envelope. Then they grabbed a taxi to the federal building.

Agent Justus Mills didn't keep them waiting long. Nicole grinned to herself—had he fulfilled the prophecy of his first name?

He shook hands with Slade and then her, raising his dark eyebrows to his bald pate. He must've been well versed in discretion, since he didn't say a peep about her presence even though she could tell he was dying to.

"I've got a room in the lab set up." Mills jerked his head toward a long hallway. "Last door on the left."

Slade and Mills walked side by side and Nicole followed them, taking quick glances right and left into the sterile, boxlike rooms they passed. What did the FBI use these for, prisoner interrogation? She really had no clue how the FBI worked. She just hoped they could give them some answers.

Mills stopped in front of a larger door than all the rest on the corridor and swiped a badge at the card reader on the wall outside. A green light beeped and the door clicked.

"This way." Mills pushed open the door and held it ajar as she and Slade scooted past him.

Now *this* looked like the FBI of her imagination. Computer servers clicked and whirred in the chilly room and intense people stared at their monitors, searching for clues in the lines of text that scrolled across their screens.

Mills led them to a room off the main lab and snapped the door shut behind him, as if to make the point that what went on out there wasn't what was going on in here.

Mills spread his fingers and pressed all ten fingertips on the table, which already contained items for lifting the prints. "You have the weapon?"

"I had to check it in when we came into the building, but you must've cleared that ahead of time, because they gave it back to me once I got through the metal detector."

"It was all cleared beforehand." Mills jerked two thumbs up at the ceiling. "Someone at a very high level is guiding this operation."

"I don't even know who that is." Slade pulled a handkerchief out of his front pocket and reached into the envelope. "I unloaded it and have tried to handle it without putting my own prints on it, but my prints are readily available if you need to check them."

"Yes, your prints have already been pulled, so they can be ruled out." Mills hunched forward and inspected the weapon Slade had placed on the table. "Nice piece. If we don't find a match here, we send the prints to Interpol. We can do domestic while you wait, but Interpol will take a few days—unless your people put a rush on it. I get the feeling it's that important."

"It is. Are you going to dust in here?"

"Yep. Dust, lift and transfer to the cards while you watch. Those are the orders I have."

"Do you mind if I sit down?" Nicole placed her hand on the back of one of the uncomfortable-looking chairs.

Mills answered, "Be my guest. The actual procedure won't take long."

She watched while Mills did the honors and Slade peppered him with questions.

"You have the capability to do the domestic match here with the computers at DOJ?"

"Right here while you wait. You can go down to the cafeteria and get some weak coffee, if you want. Your temporary badges will get you in there."

"How long will the fingerprints take?"

"Thirty minutes, maybe more, maybe less. I have your cell phone number. I'll text you whether or not we get a hit. If not, I won't hold you up, and we'll send the prints on to Interpol."

Fifteen minutes later with the fingerprinting process completed, Mills picked up the gun by the barrel. "I do have orders to keep the weapon, though."

"I know that. I got the same orders."

Nicole pushed back from the table. "Does that cafeteria have food as well as weak coffee? I could use some lunch."

"Take the elevator to the basement and you'll see the signs, or just follow the smell of grilled cheese."

"Grilled cheese?" Nicole smacked her lips. "Now that's a serious cafeteria."

Slade shook Mills's hand. "Thanks, man. I'll wait to hear from you. If it's going to Interpol, you'll let me know when those results come back?"

"I'll let you know and I'll let my superior here know. She and I are the only ones who are aware this is going down, so it must be top secret."

"Like you said, pretty high-level stuff."

Mills blew out a breath and on a rush of words, asked, "Is it true you're a Navy SEAL sniper?"

"SEALs don't operate stateside. You know that, Mills."

Ten minutes later, Nicole stood at the lunch counter, inhaling grilled cheese. "Mills wasn't kidding."

"We don't have to stay in the building. There's a whole city block out there dotted with restaurants. Those prints aren't going anywhere."

Nicole put her hands on her hips. "What? And miss out on grilled cheese sandwiches?"

She proceeded to order one with a soda while Slade opted for the weak coffee.

He paid for their food at the register while she filled up her cup with diet soda, and they wandered to a free table in the corner. Signs around the room warned of unauthorized personnel.

Nicole sized up the room beneath her lashes. "I

suppose the spooks aren't supposed to talk business in here."

"This is the FBI, not the CIA."

She picked up one half of her sandwich. "The FBI doesn't have spooks?"

"Agents, but I'm sure they're not supposed to discuss business any more than the *spooks* are."

"Or Navy SEAL snipers on secret, illegal missions."

"Illegal?" He sipped his black coffee and grimaced.

"Oh, c'mon. You know it, I know it and Mills knows it. The only ones who don't seem to know it are the guys—and the girls—who gave you this assignment."

"Oh, they know it, all right, but they think it's worth the risk of some political fallout or embarrassment."

"They can always claim national security. Isn't that what the government always does?"

"Have your years as a documentary filmmaker turned you into a conspiracy theorist?"

"I've seen my share of government conspiracies." She bit into the sandwich, her teeth crunching through the toasted bread and meeting the melted cheese inside. "Mmm, this is good."

"Just like Mom used to make?"

"Ha!" She dusted the crumbs from her fingertips onto the plate. "I just got through telling you Mom was a Vegas showgirl and then a trophy wife. She didn't do grilled cheese...or lunch, for that matter. Yours?"

"Not my mom, but Rosalinda did. She was our housekeeper and made sure I had a pretty standard childhood."

She leveled a finger at him, noticed some melted cheese on the tip and sucked it off. "That's the difference between me and you, Slade. I didn't want the normal childhood. You spent too much time feeling guilty about your family's wealth."

He threw his head back and guffawed at the ceiling. "Thanks for the psychoanalysis."

"You're welcome. Anytime." She took another bite of her sandwich and held the other half out to him. "Try it, rich boy."

Slade took a big bite that demolished almost half of the half. As he wiped his mouth with a napkin, he held up one finger. "That's my phone."

He swiped a finger across the display and sucked in a breath. "They have a match."

Chapter Eleven

Slade's heart beat double time as he and Nicole returned to the lab. Agent Mills met them at the door
and let them inside without a word.

Staring at the back of Mills's shiny, shaved head
as he followed him into the lab, Slade asked, "So,
he's domestic?"

"Sort of." He ushered them into the room where
he'd lifted the prints and snapped the door behind
them. He tapped a manila folder on the table. "It's
all in there."

Slade flipped open the folder and looked into the
eyes of the man he'd kicked in the gut last night.
"Yep, this is the guy."

"Who is he?" Nicole sidled next to him, pressing her shoulder against his, her breath coming in
short spurts.

"Marcus Friedrich. He's German, or at least he
was before he became a US citizen as a teenager."
Slade ran his finger along the sheet of paper, skim-
ming through Friedrich's life.

"German, just like Conrad, even though that's probably not Conrad's real name. What is this, a German terrorist cell?"

"Technically, Marcus is American. He moved here with his parents when he was six years old and got citizenship ten years later."

Mills cleared his throat. "Friedrich has a record—nothing big, but the fact that he was a weapons specialist in the US Army complicates things."

A white-hot flash of anger zapped Slade's body. "Someone who served in the armed forces is involved in terrorist activity? That's always the worst."

"He was dishonorably discharged, if that makes a difference." Mills cleared his throat. "Terrorist activity?"

Slade scratched his head. If Mills hadn't figured that out by now, he probably shouldn't be a special agent for the FBI. He was most likely fishing for more intel. "We don't know at this point, Mills. I'm just guessing."

"Are you supposed to go after this guy now? Call the NYPD? Call us?" Mills flicked the edge of the folder with his blunt fingers. "He has an address in New York, out in Queens."

"I'm sure I'll have my orders once I report this." Slade thrust out a hand. "Thanks, Mills. I'll take it from here."

"And I'll report back to my superior just to close the loop. Glad to help out the…US Navy."

They turned in their badges when they checked out of the building, and Slade took a deep breath when they hit the sidewalk. "We now have one name in this network. That's gotta help."

"Agent Mills seems to think Marcus is just a petty criminal."

"A petty criminal who's a weapons specialist and who chased us through a train to stop us from finding Lars's footage. He's more than a petty criminal."

"Wouldn't the FBI know that?"

"The FBI was charged with running those prints, nothing more. The agency isn't going to be looking for the same connections as the covert ops group running this show."

"So, the brain behind your assignment isn't just the CIA." Nicole waved at a taxi barreling down the street.

"Nope, but I'm not in the loop. I was sent here to protect you and gather some info."

"I'd say you're doing a lot more than gathering some info. I think once I meet Dahir tonight, we're going to blow this wide-open for this covert ops group—and they don't even have to get their hands dirty."

They stopped talking when they slid into the backseat of the cab on the way to Nicole's place.

Slade dropped Friedrich's folder in his lap. "Are you going to get your NYU sweatshirt back from Livvy?"

"I think it's a goner." She raised an eyebrow at

him. "Why, are you trying to find an excuse to visit Chanel?"

"Well, there's that, but I wouldn't mind asking Livvy a few questions." He pressed a palm against the folder. "We have a picture to show her. I'm just wondering how many guys we have out here working on this."

"I'm wondering the same thing, and they must've been set up for a while here if Trudy started dating one of them."

"Friedrich even has a place here."

"Are you going to track him down?"

"If that's what the folks upstairs want me to do. I'm going to file a report and touch base when I get back to your place, but I need to pick up my laptop first." He leaned forward, tapping on the Plexiglas separating the front seat from the back and gave the driver the new directions to Times Square.

"Laptop, shirts, toothbrush." She drummed her fingers on his thigh. "You need to pack a bag with some essentials and bring it to my mom's. Why fight it?"

He shrugged at her light tone, but she was the one fighting it—this attraction between them. Maybe it wasn't the best idea to bed the woman you were trying to protect, but he didn't want to miss his chance with her. If they didn't take this…connection between them to the next level, she might be gone from his life for good once he finished this crazy assignment.

He left Nicole waiting in the taxi while he ran up to his hotel room to grab his laptop. He shoved a few things in a small bag while he was at it. Might as well take Nicole up on her offer.

He tossed the bag on the seat between them. "Toothbrush."

By the time they got back to her mother's place, Nicole had called to check on Livvy and casually mentioned they might drop by to visit her and bring more of Chanel's toys.

Slade held the door open for Nicole as she finished the call. "She's okay with it?"

"Of course, and you can ask Livvy anything. She might think it's strange if you're questioning her about a picture, but I'm sure you can think of something."

"I don't want to impersonate a police officer, but I'll figure out something." He punched the elevator button, and when the doors opened on the floor, Slade's five senses went into overdrive.

The building seemed secure enough, but these guys were pros and there was a team of them operating to bring down Nicole. His blood pumped hot through his veins whenever he thought about the danger to Nicole's life. Maybe this high-level team of spooks should just get her out of the city and to some super-secure location, but he had a sickening suspicion that they wanted her right here to draw out this particular terror cell.

She shoved open the front door. "Do you want to check under the beds?"

"It's that obvious, huh?"

"Your face gets—" she stroked her chin "—sharp and your eyes narrow like a cat's. Your nostrils flare."

"Wow. Who knew?" He gave the downstairs a once-over anyway before setting up his laptop in the living room. "I'm going to write up some notes and send them off. Then we'll find Friedrich's address and if we're really lucky, we'll find Friedrich."

"You're not going to wait for orders to track him down?"

He shrugged. "They put me on this assignment, so I'm going to make the call."

"What'll you do with Friedrich if you find him?"

"What I couldn't do on that train—question him, and then send him somewhere else where the interrogation methods aren't quite so friendly."

"While you're doing your notes, I'm going to catch up on some emails and a little of Mom's business. You'd be surprised how much work it is to be a society doyenne—or maybe you wouldn't."

"I don't know. The way you talk about your mom makes it sound so much more interesting than what my mom does." He patted his computer. "Don't you use a laptop?"

"Just for my work when I'm in the field. I prefer the desktop in the office for the mundane tasks."

She brought him a glass of water and carried

her own toward the office. Before she disappeared through the door, she called over her shoulder, "Have fun."

Slade sent the findings on Marcus Friedrich to his contact email for Ariel and received a simple acknowledgment. He knew the covert ops agency on the other end of that email address would be turning Friedrich's life and especially his contacts upside down, but he'd have to take the initiative on this end to locate the man. He was supposed to be the muscle in this operation—the hit man, if necessary.

And if that was necessary to protect Nicole, he was all in.

When he clicked Send on the last email of the day, he stretched and downed the rest of his water. He hadn't heard one squeak out of Nicole from the office, so he put his laptop aside and strode to the office door.

She'd abandoned the desk and chair for the sofa in the corner, where she lay curled up, one arm hanging off the edge.

He crept up to the sofa and crouched next to it, studying Nicole's beautiful face, her long lashes curved on her cheek. With the lively animation smoothed out from her face, she almost looked like a different woman, someone he didn't know.

Nicole's vitality would always be a part of her appearance, the way her green eyes lit up with curiosity, the laugh lines that crinkled at the corners of her eyes, the expressive mouth that could quirk into a smile as easily as it could purse with annoyance.

Something new had crept into her face, as well—dark shadows beneath her eyes. Fatigue, worry, fear had all left their mark. He should just tuck her in right now and investigate Friedrich's home in Queens by himself. She'd be out late meeting with Dahir tonight, and she needed the sleep.

If only he could clone himself and leave his duplicate here with her, armed and ready to protect her. He could call on Leo downstairs to keep an eye on her.

He tugged on the throw blanket hanging across the back of the sofa and shook it out. As he placed it over her legs, she stirred, tucking one hand beneath her cheek.

Unfolding the blanket, he pulled it up to her chin and then stopped when he became aware of a pair of green eyes watching him. "Did I wake you?"

"Don't worry. It wasn't a deep sleep. I think the events of last night—and the night before, and was there a night before that?—finally caught up with me and hit me over the head like a somnolent sledgehammer, if you can imagine that."

"Mmm, not quite."

She squirmed up to a sitting position. "Were you going to sneak out on me?"

"I hadn't decided yet. It might be dangerous showing up at Friedrich's house."

"If he really lives there." She kicked off the blanket. "It also might be dangerous right here."

"I know. That's why I asked about a safe house for you in the report I just wrote."

"What?" She bolted upright, her eyes fully open. "A safe house? Is that like witness protection or something? I can't leave here. I'm supposed to be looking after my mother's place."

"Really? Your mom can't pay someone to do what you're doing? You're not even taking care of Chanel anymore."

"I have stuff to do, a life. My editor is working on my most recent film, and I have to be available for questions, decisions."

"And how are you going to be available for that if you're dead?"

The light faded from her eyes, and she slumped against the arm of the sofa.

Slade's gut wrenched as he watched the fire die—and he was the one who'd doused it. He grabbed her shoulders. "Someone's after you—*you*. They don't care about the film right now. They just want to make sure you don't get your hands on it. They've made that pretty clear. I don't want you getting hit by a car, shot in a park or assaulted on the train—and I can't be here forever."

Her body jerked under his grip. "What does that mean? Are you leaving? Is the shadow agency pulling you off this assignment?"

"Not yet, but that's a distinct scenario if we don't find Lars's footage, or even if we do and can't make sense of it. A Navy SEAL can't be on permanent assignment in New York City—even if I want to be." He stroked the side of her neck with his fingers.

Nicole fell into his arms, where he'd wanted her all along, and buried her face against his chest.

He threaded his fingers through the tangles in her hair as he pressed his lips against her temple. "I'm sorry. I don't want to scare you."

"Yes, you do," she murmured against his shirt. "And you should. I need to be very afraid. What did your superiors say about this safe house for me?"

Massaging the back of her neck, he said, "They haven't responded yet. They haven't responded to much of anything I've sent them."

"I get it." She pulled away from him, her eyes meeting his, almost nose to nose. "They need me, don't they?"

"What do you mean?" He shifted his gaze to a point just above her left ear.

Her delicate nostrils flared. "I thought you were into straight talk, Slade. The powers that be, Ariel, the ones pulling the strings need me here in Manhattan, searching for that film to draw out the bad guys."

"That thought did occur to me."

"Bastards."

"They did send me out here to watch over you."

"Oh, really?" She broke away from him, swinging

her legs over the edge of the sofa and nearly knocking him over. "Then why were you sneaking around my mailbox? If you were sent to look out for me, why not just approach me? I think they wanted you to watch me, all right—watch while someone tried to kill me, allowing you to move in and nab the guy after the fact and pump him for info."

Slade didn't have much of a comeback, because the same thing had occurred to him—only he'd never have allowed that to happen. He shrugged and rose to his feet. "It didn't play out that way, did it?"

"That's because whoever chose you for the assignment obviously didn't have a clue about your personality. You don't play waiting games."

"I was chosen because I saved you once, but none of my sniper teammates would've bought into that plan—which makes me believe the people at the top aren't military." He caught her hand and squeezed it. "Their original intentions don't mean I can't force them to find a safe house for you."

"I just might take you up on that offer, but right now I'm going to get ready to storm a not-so-safe house in Queens with my partner."

After changing her skirt for a pair of dark jeans and low-heeled boots, Nicole joined him in the kitchen, where he raised a banana at her.

"Hope you don't mind. I should've had one of those grilled cheese sandwiches at the FBI cafeteria."

"Help yourself. We can get some dinner after

we check out Friedrich's house and before we meet Dahir. We're just a couple of social butterflies."

"I wouldn't call these social engagements."

"Two days ago I wouldn't have, but now?" She shrugged. "It's all I got."

They took her mother's car service to Queens, since Nicole had sworn off trains for the time being, but Slade had the driver drop them off several blocks away from the address in Friedrich's criminal file.

Friedrich knew Slade had taken his weapon, knew he hadn't been wearing gloves and probably knew they'd made him from his fingerprints. Slade didn't expect the guy to be at home cooking dinner. He didn't know what to expect.

Old homes with peaked roofs and faded wood siding lined the streets in this area. An empty lot with a chain-link fence around overgrown weeds interrupted the line of houses.

If a terrorist cell was funding Friedrich's stay in New York, it hadn't gone all out for him. The rundown neighborhood had Slade checking his pocket for his gun.

"Wait." Nicole grabbed his sleeve. "Do we have a plan? The guy tried to shoot us down in a train. What's to stop him from taking potshots at us from his window as we approach the house?"

"We're not walking up to the front door and knocking. We'll approach from the side or the back, guns drawn."

"Gun—only one of us has one. What happens if a cop happens to cruise by while we're peeping in the windows with a gun out?"

"Then I use my get-out-of-jail-free card. The brass won't be happy, but they're not going to leave me hanging in the wind."

"You sure about that?" Nicole gave the chain-link fence a rattle and then continued down the sidewalk.

A block later, Slade stepped off the curb. "Let's cross the street here and do a little reconnaissance."

A few small businesses broke up the unrelenting stretch of battered residences, and Slade turned toward the first shop window and pretended to study the wares. Instead he was studying Friedrich's house in the window's reflection.

Nicole breathed heavily beside him as she discovered a newfound interest in locks and keys. "See anything?"

"Small front yard with a dumpster out front at the curb, so I don't know what that's all about. It looks like there's a path that leads to the side of the house and maybe the back. Houses aren't too close together, and the one on the right looks boarded up and abandoned."

"So, we veer to the right."

"Exactly."

"I don't see any cars out front."

"That doesn't mean anything. Are you ready, or

do you want to go into this locksmith shop and wait for me while I have a look around?"

"I'll come with you. I've come this far."

"Do as I tell you and hit the deck when I say so."

"Don't I always?"

"As a matter of fact, you do."

They backtracked down the sidewalk and then crossed the street again, approaching the house from the side. They traipsed across the lawn of the abandoned house and then followed the dried grass and weed-strewn path along the side of Friedrich's latest address.

"Gloves?" He pulled his own out of his pocket and tugged them over his hands.

Slade peered into the first window they came to, the skewed and broken blinds giving him a glimpse into an empty bedroom.

He whispered, "Looks like whoever was living here might have moved out already. He may have left a while ago."

As he sidled along the brown siding to the next window, Nicole hooked her finger in his belt loop. He cupped his hand over his eyes to look into the frosted glass of the next window. "This has to be the bathroom, and I can't see anything."

He put a hand out behind him to stop Nicole while he reached the corner of the house that led to the back. He eased around that corner and squinted at yet another dumpster. Maybe they'd tossed out a bunch of trash before they moved.

The dumpster squatted on a cracked cement patio next to a rusted-out barbecue. A sliding glass door led from the house to the patio.

He crept along the back wall with Nicole breathing down his neck. He rested his hand on his weapon inside his pocket. He didn't need any surprises coming out of that sliding door, but he'd be ready for them if they did.

Pointing to the sliding door, he said, "Look at that."

She poked her head around his shoulder. "The glass is broken."

"It looks like someone already tried to break in here."

"Not a surprise in this neighborhood." She poked his waist. "That makes it easy for us, right?"

"A little too easy."

He placed a gloved hand against the glass door and inched his fingers closer to the gaping hole. "I could reach right in here and open the door."

"Then let's do it. Maybe they didn't leave anything behind, but perhaps you can pick up more clues to their identity. The house can be dusted for prints."

Slade sawed his bottom lip with his teeth. The air felt heavy and still, and he felt like he should hold his breath for something.

"They wouldn't leave any clues like that."

Nicole stepped around him and faced the door. "Let's find out." She gripped the door handle. "You reach in there and unlock it, and I'll yank it open."

Slade placed his gloved hands against the door again, running them across the glass. He stuck one hand through the hole in the door.

As Nicole leaned back to slide open the door, the setting sun behind them glinted off the window, highlighting a silver strand running across the bottom of the door.

Nicole tugged once before Slade's adrenaline kicked in. "Stop! Get back! Get back!"

He hooked an arm around Nicole's chest and threw her body behind the dumpster on the patio.

Then the explosion behind him rocked his world.

Chapter Twelve

The ringing in her ears wouldn't stop. Between half-open eyes, she followed a billowing scrap of material on fire, floating through the air. She hoped it wouldn't land on her.

She tried to suck in a breath of air, but her lungs wouldn't expand. The air settled on her tongue instead, a dark, acrid taste filling her mouth.

She squirmed beneath the heavy, solid object on top of her but couldn't move. Had the house fallen on her, just like it had on the little pig in his flimsy wood construction?

The implacable object on top of her shifted. It spoke. It touched her face. She couldn't hear a word Slade was saying, but she didn't care. He was with her and he was safe.

Orange flames danced behind his head, illuminating his sandy-blond hair and giving it all kinds of highlights, making him look like an angel with a glowing halo.

Slade rolled off her body and hauled her to her feet. The fire from the burning house scorched the side of her face, and she turned it toward Slade's chest.

He half dragged, half carried her into the empty lot next door, over the fence downed by the blast.

Finally, she gulped in lungfuls of fresh air, or at least air that didn't have soot and particles floating in it. She glanced over her shoulder at the house consumed in flames, her gaze then darting to a cluster of people in the street.

Someone called out. "Are you okay over there?"

"We're fine. Call 911," Slade shouted back.

He hustled her through the empty lot, holding her steady as she stumbled through weeds and trash. When he got her to the sidewalk, he grabbed her shoulders and spun her toward him.

"Are you hurt, burned? How's your hearing?"

"I can hear your voice now, although my ears are ringing. I'm fine." She looked down at her jeans, which seemed to have little burn spots in them, and brushed some dirt from her skinned palms. She should've put on those gloves when Slade told her to. "I think."

Curling an arm around her waist, he said, "Thank God. Can you get on your phone and call the car service? Have him pick us up at that fast food place across the street from where he dropped us off."

"Are you hurt?" She reached up and cupped his jaw. "Your beautiful golden eyelashes are singed."

"I'm okay, and the eyelashes will grow back. Let's get the hell out of here." He grabbed her hand and strode down the sidewalk, away from the burning house and the gathering crowd—and the sirens wailing in the distance.

"How did we survive that blast, Slade?"

"I noticed the trip wire seconds before it was triggered and managed to get us behind that dumpster. A trash can saved us."

She squeezed his hand. "*You* saved us."

When they got to the corner, she pulled out her cell phone and called her mother's car service. "Give it about fifteen minutes and pick us up across the street from where you dropped us off. We'll be waiting on the sidewalk for you."

Five minutes later, they reached the fast food restaurant and Slade touched her cheek. "Go wash up a little. I'll do the same and then I'll get us something to drink. How do your lungs feel?"

She scooped in a deep breath, which caused a slight burning sensation in her lungs. "Feels like I just smoked three packs of cigarettes, but it's not that bad."

They parted ways in the short hallway containing the restrooms, and Nicole shoved through the door.

She walked to the sinks and gripped the edge of the counter as she stared into the mirror.

Black smudges marred her cheeks and her hair looked as if someone had taken a crazy hair dryer to it. Burn marks dotted her jacket, and the heels of her boots were misshapen and partially melted away.

Her body jerked as adrenaline spiked through her veins. She'd almost died in a bomb blast. She had an urge to run. Her gaze darted from mirror to mirror to mirror and the blood rushed to her head so fast she reeled with dizziness.

The nausea punched her gut, and she staggered to the first stall and threw up in the toilet. She retched a few more times and felt better for it.

Back at the sink, she said to her reflection, "If you can't run, get sick."

She filled her palm with soap from the dispenser and lathered up her hands. She washed her face and rinsed out her mouth. Then she wet down a paper towel and brushed it over the burn spots on her clothes—now she just looked trendy instead of like an escapee from a burning building.

A woman charged into the bathroom with a baby hooked to her hip and barely gave Nicole a glance. The mom busied herself with the diaper-changing station, and Nicole finished her high-end toilette by running her fingers through her tangled hair.

She left the bathroom in better shape than she'd

entered it and even managed a smile when she saw Slade by the soft drink dispenser.

He held up a cup. "Didn't know what you wanted."

"For some reason, pink lemonade sounds about right."

"You look better." He quirked an eyebrow at her. "You're gonna have to trash those jeans, though."

"Oh, I don't know." She ran a hand across her thigh, the denim of her jeans dotted with holes. "I think they look pretty fashionable."

"If you say so." He tipped his drink toward a plastic table by the window. "Let's sit down before we both collapse."

She filled her cup and grabbed a couple of napkins before joining Slade at the table. She sucked up pink lemonade, although her taste buds still seemed tainted with some chemical taste. She sloshed the drink around in her mouth.

"They were expecting us in a big way."

She nodded. "A big bang way."

"They lured us with the broken window on the sliding door, making sure we entered through the back."

"Anyone could've gone through that door. Kids. Transients in the area. The owner of the house." She rattled the ice in her cup. "They just don't care who they hurt."

"That's for sure. They would've been just as happy to nail a bunch of FBI agents as the two of us."

"Why wasn't it a bunch of FBI agents, Slade? Couldn't your unit or command force have made that happen?"

"Eventually. It would've taken the FBI a day or two at least to get the authority to descend on that house. As far as they could tell, there was no imminent danger. Friedrich is just a small-time crook who hadn't done anything lately."

"Except go after a few people on a train."

"That's off the FBI's radar. If more than just a few people at the agency knew about this operation, they could make a stink to shut it down. We have to be careful. We're stepping all over their territory."

"I hope Dahir has the goods tonight and we can put a stop to this." She folded her hands around her cup. "I've faced danger before and that kidnapping by the Somali pirates was no picnic, but this seems… more serious. I never really believed the pirates were going to kill us. They were in it for the big payoff."

"Probably." He pointed out the window. "I think that's our car. Are you sure you're up for a meeting with Dahir tonight? It could be more of the same."

"Exploding buildings? I doubt that. I told you, Dahir is loyal."

Besides, my own personal SEAL has my back.

LATER THAT EVENING after a dinner of takeout pizza and Caesar salad, Nicole stretched out on the couch and watched the flickering images on the TV of the

FDNY putting out the flames on a burning house in the Jamaica area of Queens.

She snorted as the reporter said that the cause of the blaze was still under investigation but authorities suspected arson. "Ya think?"

"The firefighters had to know from the get-go that the fire was caused by an explosive device. They're being careful about the info they're releasing. I wonder why." Slade tossed a crumpled napkin into an empty pizza box.

"What did your superiors have to say about it?" She nibbled on a piece of crust. "Did anyone ever respond to your report?"

"Nope. It's not that kind of assignment. In fact, it's not like any kind of assignment I've ever been on."

"Seems like the kind of assignment where they hang you out to dry."

"Don't worry about me." He squeezed her calf. "You're sure you want to go out and meet Dahir?"

"Of course. He may give us everything we need."

"Then we'd better get going. I want to have some time to scope out the place before he gets there—or before anyone else does."

"My guess is that nobody even knows he's here. He must've traveled on forged documents if your people don't even have a record of him entering the country. I'm sure he's here on the sly."

"We'll see, won't we?" He wagged a finger over

her stretched-out form. "You're not going to a club in that getup, are you?"

"These?" She plucked at her baggy sweatpants that she wore *only* at home, usually in private and never in front of anyone. She was getting too comfortable with Slade. "Give me fifteen minutes to change and slap on some makeup."

She slid from the couch, hiding her grimace from Slade. If she was sore now from that dive behind the dumpster, tomorrow she was going to need a whole lot of something to ease the pain.

Upstairs, she stripped out of her comfy sweats and shimmied into a pair of black leather pants. Maybe she'd gotten a little *too* comfortable in Slade's presence—not that she wanted to seduce him. Not that she *had* to seduce him. He'd been hers for the plucking last night before Dahir called, but she'd sworn off men with dangerous passions—and Slade's commitment to his SEAL team and his desire to protect his country at all costs *were* his passions.

She pulled on a lacy white camisole and buttoned a white silk blouse over it. A pair of high-heeled black booties completed her ensemble.

Now she just needed to put on some makeup, including some eyebrow pencil to fill in the brows that had been singed in the blast—wasn't that what every woman did before a night out in Manhattan?

After making up her face, she twirled her hair into

a low, loose chignon. If she was going down tonight, she'd look stylish on the descent.

She sashayed down the staircase and had the satisfaction of seeing Slade's mouth hang open for a brief second. He recovered quickly.

"You look…nice." He smacked his chest, covered by a black cotton T-shirt. "It's a good thing we're not going in together or I'd be seriously outclassed."

"The only fashion accessory you need is your big gun."

He patted the pocket of his jacket. "Got that."

"Taxi or car?"

"Let's take the car again. It's safer when I'm packing heat."

"It's also safer for a quick, discreet getaway."

"I thought you trusted Dahir?" He rolled his shoulders and winced.

"Are you in pain?"

"Nothing a couple of ibuprofen can't mask. You?"

"Oh, yeah." She stepped off the last step, brushing past him. "I'll call the car service."

A half hour later, the car stopped one block away from the club. Slade leaned forward and addressed the driver. "Ms. Hastings is waiting in the car for now. You can idle here or take a few trips around the block."

"I'll wait here for as long as I can, sir. If I'm not here when you come back, wait by the corner of that building and I'll pick you up or drop off Ms. Hastings—whatever you want."

"Thanks, Pierre." Slade liked this driver. He hadn't said one word or raised an eyebrow when he'd picked them up in Queens, slightly worse for wear than when he'd dropped them off and with sirens wailing in the distance.

Slade gave Nicole a quick, hard kiss on the mouth and a wink. "I'll do a recon and be right back."

He stepped out of the town car and jogged across the street, dodging a few taxis. He spotted the blue awning of the club up ahead and cut over a block early. All these places had to have side or back entrances to meet fire regulations.

He slipped into an alley and maneuvered around a few dumpsters. The dark blue building that housed The Blues Joint stood out from the rest, and Slade approached the back entrance.

He tried the door handle, but it didn't budge. He pounded on the metal door with his fist.

A minute later it cracked open and an eyeball traveled the length of his body and back again. "The entrance is around the front—and there's a cover charge."

"I'd be happy to pay the cover charge, but I'm wondering if I can come in this way and look around for a place to position myself."

The door opened wider and a substantial-looking

African-American man stared him down. "Position yourself for what?"

"I have a client coming in here later and I don't want to be in the way. You understand?"

"No." The man folded his arms, resting them on his massive belly. "What kind of client?"

"I'm a bodyguard. My client's a top model." He shrugged. "You know, probably delusions of grandeur. Nobody would notice her anyway, but she's borrowing some pretty expensive jewelry tonight and I'm supposed to watch over her. I don't want to create a scene. You feel me?"

The man puffed out his cheeks for a few seconds.

"I mean, the broad's willing to pay for it." Slade pulled a wad of bills from his pocket and slipped it into the other man's hand. "I'm Nick."

"Eli." The cash disappeared as Eli dipped his head. "Yeah, sure."

The door widened and Slade squeezed past Eli, who hadn't exactly given him a wide berth. Slade hesitated at the top of a staircase. "Where does this lead?"

"That goes down to the club. This level has a small dining area around the front. We don't allow food downstairs, but some patrons come early for the show, have a meal and head down to hear the music."

"Can you see the club from the stairs?"

Eli leveled one finger in the direction of the staircase. "Help yourself."

Slade ducked beneath the low ceiling and jogged down the stairs. At the first landing, he got a full view of the club, already half-full with the band tuning their instruments on the stage. Was Dahir already here?

He scanned the patrons, but didn't see anyone resembling Dahir. The meeting was in another forty-five minutes, and Slade planned to camp out right here to watch Nicole.

He went back up the stairs and met Eli at the top. "The main entrance leads right to the club, right?"

"Yeah, that's street level in the front."

"Are many more diners going to head this way?"

"A few."

Slade took another couple of bills from his pocket. "Okay if I station myself on the landing? I think I already paid the cover charge, and if there's a drink minimum, I'll order a coffee."

Eli stuffed the money in the front pocket of his black shirt. "I think this takes care of the drinks, too. But if there's any trouble in here? I never saw you or spoke to you, and I have no idea how you got in here. You feel *me*?"

"Absolutely." Slade retreated to a pantry off the kitchen and called Nicole.

"Where are you?"

"I'm in the club, in the kitchen. I have the perfect lookout perch to watch you. I don't think Dahir is here yet, but if he's here when you arrive and he's sitting too close to the stage, ask if you can move toward the front of the club, closer to the door. I don't have a clear view of the tables ringing the stage."

"Okay, I can do that. You're not coming back to the car?"

"No, I'm good here. Oh, and you're some top model who's wearing some expensive jewelry."

"What?"

"I had to concoct some story to get in here. You're a real diva who thinks she deserves protection."

Nicole laughed her bubbling laugh, born of years of private schools, financial security and confidence. He'd heard it a million times on the lips of the girls he was expected to date, but Nicole's confidence came from living in the real world. Her self-assuredness came from a belief in her work. In short, she was nothing like the girls he'd grown up with.

"I can play that role to a T, rich boy, but you should've warned me. I could've piled on some of my mom's jewelry to really get into character."

"That's okay. There's only one guy we need to convince, and I'm pretty sure I already did that with a wad of cash."

"Okay, so what do I do for the next half hour?"

"Have Pierre take you on a sightseeing tour around Harlem. Whatever you do, have him drop you off in front of the club at eleven o'clock and go straight inside."

"Gotcha. I'm actually looking forward to seeing

Dahir. I haven't seen him since we all left that Navy boat after our rescue."

"I hope it's the reunion you expect—and not something else."

Nicole cleared her throat. "Should we have some sort of signal in case things start heading south?"

"You're getting good at this espionage stuff. Get a drink, make sure it has a straw, and if you need help, stick the straw in your mouth and flick it with your finger. That's not something you'd do naturally, but it wouldn't seem odd if someone did do that."

"Really? Shoving a straw in your mouth and flicking it around isn't odd?"

"You have a better idea, Ms. Bond?"

"My hair's up. If I sense something hinky, I'll let my hair down."

"What if it falls down by accident?"

"It's not going to do that. Trust me."

"I do trust you, Nicole Hastings, and I'll be watching you in about a half an hour." He ended the call and stayed put in the corner of the pantry.

The band had started playing and their smooth jazz tones floated up the staircase, luring more diners from the restaurant. About twenty minutes later, Slade eased out of his position and crept downstairs.

Hearing a heavy footfall behind him, Slade spun around and Eli almost took him out with a stool.

"Whoa, my man. I was just bringing you something to sit on."

"Sorry, thanks. I'll take it." He gripped one leg of the stool and continued down the last few steps. He tucked the stool in the corner of the landing and straddled it.

Eli had joined him on the landing. "You need anything else?"

"I'm good." Slade pointed across the room at another landing. "What's over there?"

"Bathrooms, accessible from another staircase near the stage." Eli poked his shoulder. "Is that your girl?"

Slade glanced down at Nicole floating through the room, her loose white blouse billowing behind her. He held his breath as she continued toward the stage, finally stopping at a table in the corner but still within his line of sight. He eased out a breath.

"Yep, that's her."

"I could tell. She's definitely supermodel material."

"Yeah, she is."

"I'll leave you to it, man." Eli snapped his fingers and pointed at him. "Remember, if anything goes down, I don't know you."

"Never saw you before in my life."

Eli hauled his considerable girth downstairs to the club.

Slade shifted his gaze to Nicole, and his heart stuttered when a man joined her at the table. If he had his rifle and scope, he could zero on him and get a better look.

Nicole jumped up from her seat and threw her arms around the man, who was half a head shorter than she was.

Slade rolled his shoulders. Had to be Dahir.

The translator glanced over his shoulder once and took a seat, facing the front door. The man wasn't taking any chances.

Nicole and Dahir hunched toward each other, presumably to catch each other's words over the wail of a trumpet. Slade's heart thumped in time with the syncopated rhythm of the drums as he watched Nicole and Dahir through narrowed eyes.

Just get the goods and get out.

Dahir had pulled out his phone, and Slade responded by flicking the safety from his gun and dragging it out of his pocket.

With their heads together, Nicole and Dahir studied the phone. Maybe he was showing her the footage and explaining its significance. Then they could get out of here.

Slade licked his dry lips, feeling more like he was on a sniper detail in Iraq than sitting in a jazz club in Harlem. The hair on the back of his neck refused to stop quivering. His jaw refused to unlock.

Two drinks magically appeared on the small table between Nicole and Dahir, and all his senses ratcheted up another notch. Had he missed the waiter taking their order?

Maybe Nicole had ordered something when she first walked in the door.

Slade kept an eye on the bun on the back of Nicole's head—still in place as she smiled and nodded over the phone. She wouldn't be so happy if Dahir were showing her that footage. She must be looking at pictures, but she needed to get down to business.

And then something changed.

As Nicole reached for her glass, there was a sharp movement from across the table and it crashed to the floor. The noise and activity drew a few glances from the other patrons nearby, but the band seemed to drown out the sound for most of the other customers.

As Nicole bent forward to pick up the shards of glass, Dahir shot up from his seat and tilted his head back to take in the landing across the way.

With a rush of adrenaline, Slade jerked his head toward the other staircase by the bathrooms. The barrel of a weapon glinted in the lights.

Slade hopped up from the stool, swinging his gun toward the threat across the room, but he was too late.

A flash of light lit up the landing as the man fired into the club below—and the fight was on.

Chapter Thirteen

As Nicole started to sit up, she heard a thwack above her. She knew the sound—she'd heard it around the world. She slid from her chair and dropped beneath the small cocktail table.

A split second later, Dahir fell to the floor next to her, copious amounts of blood leaking from a bullet hole in his forehead.

A few people screamed, but the music continued, the band unaware of the drama unfolding in the club, their dissonant chords matching the confusion raging through Nicole's brain.

Slade couldn't be responsible for Dahir's death. She hadn't signaled anything, had been aware of nothing amiss as Dahir shared pictures of his family back in Somalia.

If not Slade, then some other shooter—someone hostile.

Dahir's blood continued to soak the club's dark blue carpet and slowly more and more patrons understood just why the man at her table had dropped like a rock.

Chaos erupted all at once as a collective realization hit. And then something else hit—the back of the chair where she'd just been sitting splintered into pieces as another bullet made contact.

She flattened herself on the floor and started crawling toward the front door. A few people stepped on her during the stampede for the exit, but others joined her in a slithering journey to safety.

A crack and a thud behind her, toward the stage, didn't slow her path, but someone yelled, "He's been hit. The shooter's been hit."

The shooter? Which one? Slade was up there, too. Had he been hit?

Nicole couldn't breathe for the second time that day, but this time fear instead of smoke clogged her lungs. She scrabbled against the carpet, turning herself around to head back toward the stage.

She reached forward with one hand and hit a shoe. Seconds later, Slade was on the floor next to her, nose to nose.

"You're going the wrong way. Stay down and keep moving for the exit. I got him, but I don't know if there's anyone else in here gunning for you."

They shimmied on the carpet next to each other until they reached the door. Slade pulled her outside and she drank in the evening air with big gulps.

This time they got away before they even heard

a hint of sirens, running down the sidewalk with a crowd of other people escaping the mayhem in the club.

After traveling a city block, gasping for breath at the fast pace Slade set, Nicole pulled on his arm. "Should I call for the car now?"

He glanced at her hand on his sleeve and sucked in a breath. "You're bleeding. You're hurt."

Turning her hand over, she inspected the cut on her fingers. "It's from the broken glass that Dahir knocked over."

"Right before the shot that killed him."

"I think I know what happened." She curled her fingers over the blood smudged on her hand. "Dahir brought those drinks to the table with him, and before I could even take a sip of mine, he knocked it over."

"What are you saying? Do you think there was something in the drink?"

"I'm not sure, but he was nervous even when he was showing me pictures of his family." She retrieved her phone. "I'm calling for the car."

Pierre must've been close, because less than ten minutes later, the black town car cruised up to the curb. They both piled in and Nicole slumped in the seat, her head tilted back.

A few hot tears coursed down her face and she dashed them away. They had an agreement to keep mum in front of Pierre and any other driver, although he must have his suspicions. She didn't need to involve anyone else in the train wreck of her life. Anyone within two feet of her was entering some sort of death zone.

Silently, they made it back to her mother's place, and as soon as she double locked the door behind them, she let loose. "Dahir saved me, Slade."

"Maybe, but why did he lure you to that club in the first place? It's obvious the second bullet had your name on it. The shooter's mistake was killing Dahir first. I guess he figured you'd pop up and he could take care of you next."

She marched to the kitchen and perched on the edge of a stool at the island. "His mistake was not realizing there was another sniper in that club. You're sure you got him?"

"I almost shot him before he nailed Dahir. I saw him, or rather his weapon, when Dahir looked up in his direction after knocking over that drink. I got my shot off right after he killed Dahir and got off his second shot. Thank God you were still on the floor."

"That proves it."

"Proves what?" He joined her at the counter and tapped the back of her injured hand. "Let me clean that up for you."

She stretched out her palm for him as he ran a paper towel beneath the faucet and squirted some soap on it.

"Once Dahir knocked over my drink, he knew he'd signed his death warrant."

"Then why'd he come all this way to find you and do their bidding? What's clear is that this was a setup, orchestrated by the people after you and using Dahir to get to you." He dabbed at the dried blood on her hand and swiped the paper towel over the cut, which had bled out of proportion to its size.

"I can't explain that. Maybe he had a change of heart once we saw each other again. He was showing me pictures of his family back in Somalia." She bolted forward and grabbed Slade's wrist. "His family. That's how they got to him."

"Do you think they're threatening his family?" He slipped out of her grasp, dumped the bloody paper towel in the trash and grabbed a dry one. He pressed it to her cut.

"I know they're threatening his family." She snapped her fingers several times in a row. "One of the things he said to me was that he hoped I could protect or do something for his family if anything happened to him."

"So, the group used his family to get him to lure you out."

"Can you help them, Slade? Please. We owe him this."

"Do we? While I understand his motivation, he put your life in danger. He should've contacted us *before* he set you up."

"Really?" She crumpled the paper towel in her fist and jerked back from him. "I told you I tried to help him before with no success whatsoever, thanks to you guys."

"Us guys?" He held up his hands. "Don't blame me."

"I'm gonna blame you now if you can't do something for his family. He saved my life. I'm sure of that."

"I'll get on it. Or at least I'll relay the information to the people who can actually do something about it." He pulled up a stool and sat beside her.

"I'm sorry." She rubbed her knuckles across the soft denim covering his thigh. "I didn't mean to blame you. I'm just so devastated by Dahir's murder. That means everyone who was on that boat in the Gulf of Aden is dead—except me."

He covered her hand with his. "We're going to keep it that way. Did he tell you anything about the footage, what was on it?"

"We didn't even get that far. He just said that I probably knew why we were meeting."

"Maybe he didn't even know why that film is so important." Slade closed his eyes and pinched the bridge of his nose. "This brings us back to the key and the search for that locker. It's the best lead we've had yet and I allowed myself to get distracted by other issues that resulted in nothing."

"We couldn't have searched for the locker anyway with Luna Park being closed, and it's not like I could've ignored a meeting with Dahir."

"No, but I had a strong suspicion it was a trap, and I shouldn't have let you go through with it. I could've met with him instead."

"You're not trying to blame yourself for what happened, are you?" She touched his face. "Dahir would never have gone for that…and neither would your superiors. They need me to bring these people out of the woodwork, and we both know it."

Slade captured her uninjured hand, threading his fingers through hers. "That was never my plan. I hope you know that."

She pressed her palm against his. "I do, and I even understand the perspective of the people running the show."

"How did such a pampered girl like you—" he drew her hand toward him and kissed her wrist "—get so tough? I saw it on that pirate boat and I see it over and over again here."

Leaning forward, she rested her forehead against his. "I'm not that tough, Slade. Just like on that pirate boat, I have you as my backup. You give me strength."

He cupped her face, his fingers toying with her earlobe. "And you make this assignment worthwhile."

Worthwhile. The word echoed in her head and struck a chord in her heart. That was the difference between Slade and all the other thrill seekers in her past.

Slade took his risks for a purpose. He worked for a greater good beyond that of his own ego.

She turned her face toward the hand cupping her jaw and pressed a kiss on his palm, roughened by the work he did protecting others…protecting her.

Their eyes met, and along with the usual electricity that flashed between them, there was a hint of understanding, of acceptance.

She wasn't the spoiled rich girl type he'd come to loathe, and he wasn't the irresponsible risk taker who put himself above everything else, above her.

Slade would never put his needs above hers.

Tipping forward on two legs of his stool, he brushed a thumb across her lips and then kissed her mouth.

She nodded toward the floor. "You're going to fall off that thing."

"Then let's take this to solid ground." The stool fell back as he rose to his feet. He cinched her waist with both hands and pulled her up and against him in a gentle embrace. "I'm not carrying you this time. You come of your own free will…or not at all."

He released her and turned his back on her but before he even got out of the kitchen, she ran up behind him and wrapped her arms around his waist, resting her head against his strong back—a back that carried the weight of the world, the protection of innocent people everywhere, of her.

Without turning around, he squared his shoulders and said, "When this is over, I go back to doing what I do."

"I wouldn't have it any other way. You're a warrior." She hugged him tighter, hugged him as if her life depended on it.

He turned in her arms and brushed the hair from her face. He kissed her temple, her cheekbone, her ear, her chin. "Then you're my warrior princess, Nicole Hastings."

How they ended up on the floor in front of the fireplace, naked and breathless, their limbs entwined and tangled, she couldn't exactly remember. She only knew nothing had ever felt so right.

After another long kiss in a mind-swirling number of long kisses, Nicole straddled Slade, running her hands along the hard planes and ridges of his body. "Are all SEALs built like you?"

"Absolutely not. I'm a prime specimen." He stroked her thigh, his rough hands abrading her skin. "And I hope you just take my word for it and that ends your curiosity about any other SEAL you might encounter."

She leaned forward, brushing the tips of her breasts along his chest. "I have no curiosity about any other man... SEAL or otherwise."

He cupped her bottom with both hands, kneading

her flesh, urging her forward until her face hovered above his. Slade's tongue tickled her earlobe and then he bared his teeth against her collarbone.

She gave a little shiver at the contrast between soft and hard. Although Slade's body didn't seem to have one soft spot on it, except for his lips, he had a surprisingly tender touch. Those lips pressed against her throat as if measuring her erratic pulse.

His hands slid up her back. "Are you cold?"

"No—excited." She bent her head and tickled his chest with the ends of her hair.

"Me, too."

As she wriggled against his hard erection, she gave him her best wicked grin. "I can tell."

He closed his eyes, catching his breath. "That feels so…good, which is a really weak word for what I'm experiencing right now."

She shifted her body to the side, not wanting this to end too soon, and trailed her fingernails across his chest. Now it was his turn to shiver.

"Are *you* cold?"

"I'm so hot I'm surprised I don't have steam coming out of my ears."

"Who says?" She flicked his earlobe with her tongue, and he chuckled.

He pulled her down next to him and pressed the length of his body against hers, their flesh meeting along every line. His breath was hot and heavy on her cheek.

The adrenaline and heightened sense of awareness that had been flashing through her body ever since the shooting at the club hadn't subsided. Every touch from Slade set fire to her skin and engendered a hunger deep in her soul that she couldn't seem to satisfy, no matter how many times she explored his body or indulged in his kisses.

"I want more of you." She slid down his body, burying her head between his thighs, taking him into her mouth.

He bucked against her, and his fingers dug into her scalp. "You could've warned me. My head just about exploded."

She replaced her mouth with her hand, stroking the tight flesh that she'd moistened with her tongue. "Is that a double entendre?"

"Why are you asking me questions now, in French, no less? Just keep doing whatever it is you were doing down there."

"Aye, aye, Captain." She dabbled the tip of her tongue along the insides of his thighs—didn't want his head exploding too fast—and then closed her lips around his girth once again.

Slade shuddered and moaned, teasing her hair into a tangled mess with his fingers. When she started getting creative, he clamped his hands on her shoulders.

"We're finishing this another way."

She worked her way up his body with kisses until

she met his mouth. She whispered against his lips, "I'm all yours."

And at this particular moment, she meant it.

Flipping her onto her back, he answered gruffly, "And I've been all yours from the minute I saw you through my scope."

She braced for the onslaught of this hard-as-nails man, but he turned tender on her again by kissing her eyelids and smoothing one large hand over her breast, his fingertips toying with her nipple.

She clawed at his backside, desperate for him to be inside her, desperate for him to slake her need.

He prodded her, opening her slowly, filling her up. Her passion rose swiftly as he claimed her inch by inch, until her head thrashed from side to side with the wanting of him.

Driving into her to the very hilt, he growled, "Is this what you want?"

Did he expect her to form words? Actual thoughts? All she could do was wrap her legs around his hips and go along for the ride—and what a ride it was.

As hard as he'd been in her mouth, she'd expected him to reach his climax almost immediately…but the man had tricks and he exulted in using them on her, bringing her to heights of desire only to leave her at the precipice, almost weeping with frustration.

Then he stopped fooling around and got down to business. He scooped his hands beneath her derriere, tilting her hips upward. He must've been paying attention to her responses because when he took her this way, the fluttering in her belly threatened to overcome her.

The rhythm of their bodies as they connected and then pulled apart put her into a trance, and she couldn't think anymore. Her nerve endings throbbed and pulsed, and all the muscles in her body tensed once before her orgasm roared through her.

She thought it would never end, and then Slade had his own release, and the pounding of his flesh against hers made her toes curl and her body turn to jelly. She tried to clamp herself around him, tried to increase his pleasure, but she felt boneless and weightless.

All the teasing, all the buildup, all the waiting had resulted in a climax that had drained her of all reason.

He kissed her mouth before he rolled to his side next to her, closing his eyes.

She panted beside him, waiting for the trembling of her limbs to subside. He'd just taken her someplace she'd never even imagined—and she wanted to go back there again and again.

She smoothed her hand along his damp shoulder and followed her touch with a kiss. "Is it just me, or was that mind-blowing sex?"

"I was thinking the same thing, wondering, does she have sex like this all the time? Like a freight train blasting over you at a hundred miles an hour. Like some spell where all you can do is feel and every sense is in overdrive."

"Took the words right out of my mouth." She tried to pinch his waist, which was next to impossible as he didn't seem to have an ounce of fat on him. "You're not lying to me, are you?"

"Look at me." He poked a finger against his flat belly. "I'm a mess—in the best possible way, but I'm drained."

She touched her tongue to his salty nipple. "You don't look like a mess to me. In fact, I want a keepsake of this moment."

He raised his eyebrows. "What do you have in mind?"

"Just one little picture...or two." She crawled from their makeshift bed on the floor toward her purse on the chair. "I swear my phone will never be hacked. Your picture will never wind up online."

"What kind of pictures are we talking about here?" He scrunched up a pillow behind his head and punched it a few times to watch her progress.

"Let's just go with it." She grabbed the strap of her purse and yanked it from the chair. It fell open on the floor, scattering its contents. Spying her phone in the jumble, she grabbed it. As she picked it up, she scooped up a cocktail napkin at the same time.

"What's this doing in my purse?" She held it up between two fingers like a white flag.

Slade squinted in her direction. "It's from The Blues Joint."

Then she saw the writing on the back of the napkin, along with a spot of blood. Her heart pounding, she smoothed the napkin against her knee. "Slade, Dahir left me a note before he died."

Chapter Fourteen

Slade shot up, scrambling to join Nicole next to the contents of her purse. "Does the note say where the film is?"

"Ah, no." She pinched the napkin by its corners and turned it toward him, swinging it in front of his face. "It's a bunch of numbers—fifteen, twenty-three, nineteen."

He poked the napkin with his finger. "What the hell does that mean? A combination?"

"We already have a key. We don't need a combination, too."

"A time? Three twenty-three, maybe?"

"You're seriously asking me? I don't have a clue, Slade—or rather, I only have a clue." She waved the napkin. "This one."

"We need to find some lockers at Coney Island tomorrow. There just might be a combination lock as well. It's our best chance of finding the film. Once we get it, we're going to have to figure out what we have quickly. The film itself isn't going to do us any good if we don't know the significance of what's on it."

"And the CIA or this Ariel person is going to have to act fast on the info, because if we have the film and don't know the importance of what we're holding, this terrorist cell is still going to try to get it back before we can figure it out and take action. Right?"

"You're right." He creased one corner of the cocktail napkin. "Hang on to this. Dahir went through a lot of trouble to write this down for you. It has to mean something."

Nicole covered her white face with one shaky hand. "Here I am having sex on the same night my friend and coworker is murdered. I feel…"

"Hey." He wedged a knuckle beneath her chin and tilted up her head. "That's what happens sometimes after the heat of the fight. We're riding high, the adrenaline is pumping. We need an outlet, a release. Your feelings were natural, and they don't mean Dahir or his death means less to you."

"I'm spent. I can barely lift a finger." She raised her hand to test out her theory.

"It's all hitting you now. You're coming down from the rush." He dragged the blanket from the floor and draped it over Nicole's shoulders. "It's my fault. I knew what you were probably experiencing and I shouldn't have taken advantage of your state.

It's almost like taking advantage of someone when they're drunk."

Her head snapped up. "Stop. I knew what I was doing. I don't want you to think I regret what happened between us, because I don't. It's just that... I think I need to feel sad now. I mean, I *am* sad."

"Like I said." He cinched the blanket beneath her chin. "You're coming down hard—and I'm going to be right next to you when you hit the bottom."

Her eyes filled with tears, and she leaned her forehead against his chest.

"Let's get to bed." He stroked her hair and kissed the top of her head. Then he pushed to his feet and put the napkin with Dahir's cryptic message on the counter, wedging it beneath the telephone. "Do you want your phone charging down here or in your room?"

She sniffed. "I'll take it up."

While she shoved items back into her purse, Slade tossed the pillow back on the couch, not sorry he wouldn't be spending another night there.

He pulled on his boxers and bunched up the rest of his clothes under one arm.

Nicole hadn't been kidding. Her slow movements indicated lethargy, and as she crouched down to gather her own scattered clothing, she nearly fell over.

"Whoa." He caught her. "Let me get those for you

and lock up down here. You get up to bed and don't worry about anything."

As she plodded upstairs, clutching her clothes to her chest, he checked the doors and windows and hit the lights. Nicole had let the blanket slip from her shoulders, so he folded that up and placed it on his former bed.

Then he washed a few dishes in the sink and filled up a glass with water. By the time he got to Nicole's bedroom, she'd burrowed under the covers, leaving the light on in the connecting bathroom.

He brushed his teeth and splashed some water on his face and then crawled between the sheets next to Nicole.

He spooned her naked body against his, kissing the side of her neck.

She sighed. "I really don't regret making love with you, Slade, because that's what we did, isn't it? We made love, and it made me feel whole and safe and alive."

"We made love, Nicole."

And God help him, he meant it.

THE NEXT MORNING, Slade wrapped his arms around Nicole as he'd done all night, and then realized he had a cool pillow instead of a hot woman in his embrace.

He opened one eye, peering at the light coming through a gap in the drapes. Nicole didn't have an alarm clock in here and he'd left his cell phone downstairs, but that light at the window meant he'd slept through a good portion of the morning.

He rolled out of the bed and stretched. A light floral scent wafted from the bathroom. Nicole had managed to shower and get dressed and he'd slept through it all. What a bodyguard.

A sliver of fear pricked the back of his neck, just like it did whenever Nicole was out of his line of vision. He jogged downstairs, calling her name.

Poking her head out of the kitchen, she said, "What's all the racket?"

His pulse returned to normal. "You're up early."

"I couldn't sleep. You were right when you said the events of last night would hit me, they did—like a sledgehammer." She pointed to the TV. "There was a story on the shooting. It's all very vague. They haven't identified the gunman yet."

"Our FBI contact will move in on that one, and hopefully we can ID another member of this cell."

Nicole had made coffee, and the smell perked up his senses. His head still felt groggy, almost as if he'd taken that drink meant for Nicole last night. But he didn't need to take anything—Nicole Hastings was his drug of choice, and he didn't think he could ever OD on her.

She poured him a cup of coffee, her head tilted to one side. "You okay?"

"A little groggy. I feel stupid that I slept through

everything this morning when I'm supposed to be protecting you. Usually, I'm a light sleeper."

"I guess that's the danger of mixing business and pleasure." She buried her head in the fridge.

He narrowed his eyes as he took a sip of coffee. Was she back to regretting their hookup? No, she'd been right last night. That was no hookup. Maybe she was regretting the depth of feeling on both sides. She'd hinted her next man was going to be the buttoned-down type.

He'd vowed never to get involved with a rich society woman, but after meeting Nicole, he'd learned not to generalize. Maybe she needed to give him a chance, too.

She popped out of the fridge holding an egg in each hand. "Do you want some breakfast before we check out those lockers?"

"Yeah, but do you mind if we go out to eat? I'm getting sick of my scrambled eggs."

"I'm sorry, I'm not much of a breakfast person."

"You weren't exactly expecting guests, either." He picked up his coffee cup and sat down on the sofa in front of his laptop, charging on the coffee table. "I'm going to check my messages and see if Ariel got back to me on Dahir's family and the ID of the shooter last night."

"I'll give Livvy a call and check on Mom's dog."

Slade powered up his computer. "Ask her if the

cops have a lead on the driver or car, especially since we haven't had a chance to talk to her yet."

"I think we've been a little busy."

He launched his secure email, and a flurry of messages scrolled by. His gut knotted as he clicked on the first email from Ariel.

It was short and not so sweet, like most of her communications. Dahir's family missing.

Slade glanced over the top of his laptop at Nicole perched on a stool chatting with Livvy on the phone. She didn't need to know this information right now, even though it might make her feel slightly better that Dahir hadn't betrayed her. Dahir *had* been trying to protect his family—but she'd figured that out all on her own.

This terrorist cell was powerful and far-reaching enough to have operatives in New York and still be able to kidnap a family in Somalia.

Vlad—his sniper team's nemesis in Afghanistan—could he have developed a network like this? Slade double clicked on the next email, which contained slightly better news.

Nicole had ended her call to Livvy and was watching him with her eyebrows raised. "Well?"

"The FBI ID'd the shooter from last night—Phillipe Moreau."

"A Frenchman?"

"An elite sniper, a gun for hire."

"No allegiance to a particular group or country?"

"Not that we know of." Rubbing his chin, he squinted at the picture of Moreau that Ariel had attached to the email. "That could've changed. And that exploding house yesterday?"

"Yeah?"

"Bomb-making factory—the whole house. That's what Marcus Friedrich was doing there, so it wasn't a big step for him to rig that door with an explosive."

She cupped her face with both hands. "Oh, my God, right out there in Queens? Who knows how many other attacks they've been planning?"

"Their operation seems like a well-oiled machine to me. That's why this footage puzzles me. What could be so important that they'd put other projects on hold to get this film?"

"Hopefully, we're on the verge of discovering that." Nicole hunched forward slightly and he held his breath. She asked the dreaded question. "Dahir's family? Any news on them?"

"Not yet." He skimmed through the remaining emails and closed down his laptop. "I'm going to shower and change—and we don't even have to drop by my hotel."

"Then we'll feed you and take a trip to Coney Island."

"Can we take the car service out there? I think that's the safest way to go—no more shooters on trains, and let's get Pierre again since we know him."

"It's fine. I think I mentioned my mom has that

service on retainer, so she's charged for it whether we use it or not."

"Ah, money."

She shook a finger at him. "Don't tell me you don't have something similar, rich boy."

"In California we don't have car services. We just have cars—and lots of 'em."

"At your place, we'd just survey the garage and eenie-meenie-miney-moe between the Lambo, the Ferrari and the Maybach."

"The Porsche—don't forget the Porsche." Slade stashed his laptop beneath the coffee table and bounded up from the sofa. "Give me fifteen minutes."

He dashed upstairs and past the bed with its rumpled bedclothes to the cavernous bathroom. He took a quick shower, trying not to think of the night he'd spent with Nicole.

In the harsh light of day with a man's family missing, he had to put his feelings about Nicole on the back burner. That's exactly how it felt, deep in his soul, simmering on a back burner, still warm, still stirring his blood.

He decreased the water temperature in the shower and finished rinsing off in a lukewarm spray. He got dressed in record time, just in case Nicole got any bright ideas about barging in on him—because he had no willpower to resist her.

When he made it downstairs, Nicole was on the

phone again, and she waved at him as she continued talking. "Chanel is fine, Mom. She sort of saved Livvy's life. She's a hero."

Nicole rolled her eyes at him. "I just thought Livvy could use the extra income right now since she can't exactly walk dogs. Chanel will be fine over there. I'll bring her back home after…in a little while."

Nicole listened to her mother for a very long time, all the while making faces. "Love you, too, Mom. Have a great time and don't worry about a thing. Everything's under control."

She ended the call with a sigh. "That woman could talk your ear off."

"Everything's under control? That couldn't be farther from the truth."

Nicole lifted her shoulders. "What she doesn't know can't hurt her."

Amen to that.

NICOLE SLID INTO the backseat of the town car and Slade followed her, nodding to Pierre as he held the door open.

When the car lurched away from the curb, Slade turned to her. "It's not very warm out. Do you think there will be many people there?"

"Not as crowded as summertime, obviously, but there are arcades and shows and other things to do there besides go to the beach."

Slade bobbled the key in the palm of his hand. "I have a good feeling about this—we have proof that Lars and Trudy went to Coney Island, and Trudy mentioned a key before she died, and this is definitely no ordinary key."

"Yeah, but we don't even know if Coney Island has these kinds of lockers, and if it does, how long will it take us to try every locker?"

"Don't be so pessimistic. You said it yourself. It won't be that crowded, so maybe not many people using the lockers this time of year. I'm sure there will be plenty of lockers with their keys intact, and we can bypass those."

She tilted her head at him. "You *are* feeling confident. I like it."

After crawling through traffic in Manhattan, the car moved faster once they hit Brooklyn. It was still almost an hour before Pierre rolled through the parking lot of the beachside amusement park.

Slade tapped on the darkly tinted glass that separated driver from passenger, and the partition magically slid open. "Pierre, can you pick us up here? I'm not sure how long we'll be, but Nicole will text you when we're ready in case you want to leave and come back."

"I'll probably stay here, sir, although it's been a while since I had a corn dog."

Nicole laughed. "We'll get you one."

As Pierre made a move to get out of the car, Slade

stopped him. "We can manage. You don't have to keep hopping in and out of the car to open the door for us."

Nicole jabbed him in the back as he exited the car, but he ignored her. She'd never felt guilty about her family's wealth because her parents had managed to do so much good with it. Maybe Slade's parents weren't as generous with their money.

She could probably get a better sense of them and what made Slade tick once she met them. She tripped, the toe of her sneaker catching the edge of the curb. *If* she ever met them.

Slade caught her arm. "Careful."

Inhaling a deep breath of salty air, she said, "This way."

They bought tickets for the amusement park, since it was the only way to get inside, and wandered around the entrance area looking for lockers, without any luck.

Wedging her hands on her hips, Nicole said, "We should've just asked when we bought the tickets."

"I didn't think we'd have to. I thought they'd be right up front with the bathrooms and the stroller rentals."

"Men never ask about anything important." She marched back to the ticket counter and grabbed the first attendant she saw. "Excuse me, do you have lockers here? You know, maybe for a purse?"

"Sorry, no lockers here."

Her shoulders slumped and she made a half turn before the attendant called after her. "But Luna Park next door has lockers."

Her head snapped up. "We don't have to pay to get in there, do we?"

"No, just for the individual rides."

"Thanks." She grabbed Slade's arm and dragged him toward the front of the park. "Renewed hope."

They wandered into Luna Park, which had signs all around announcing its opening for the season.

Slade uttered an expletive and grabbed her arm. "Nicole, this is their opening weekend."

"I know. We lucked out."

"No, we didn't." He shook his head. "If Luna Park wasn't open last month, how would Lars and Trudy have been able to get a locker here?"

"Oh." She bit her lip but refused to lose hope. "Maybe they didn't have to get inside to get a locker. Let's ask first this time."

She approached a park worker who was sweeping up popcorn. "Excuse me. Where are the lockers?"

"Back by the ticket kiosk." He jerked a thumb over his shoulder.

Nicole shook off Slade's hold and skipped ahead. When she reached the kiosk, she tripped to a stop and spit out the same expletive Slade had chosen earlier.

He almost bumped into her and then whistled when he surveyed the rows of blue lockers facing them—electronic lockers, not a keyhole in sight.

The woman at the ticket counter poked her head forward. "If you want to rent a locker, you need to buy a card and the card works on the lockers."

Nicole swore under her breath again, and the ticket seller raised her eyebrows.

"No keys?" Slade pulled Trudy's key from his pocket. "Like this?"

The woman squinted her eyes. "No. All our lockers are electronic now."

Dead end.

Blowing out a breath, Slade pocketed the key and took Nicole's hand. "Maybe we should check out those lockers at the Statue of Liberty you mentioned."

"There are some old-style lockers by the beach."

Nicole glanced up at the kid still pushing his broom at imaginary dirt and poked Slade.

He showed him Trudy's key. "You mean like this? With a key?"

"Yeah. There are a couple of rows of them, right beneath the boardwalk. You stick in some quarters and you can pull out the key. I think they're going to be destroyed, but they're still there."

"Thanks."

They exchanged one look and then rushed from Luna Park as if they'd just been on the tilt-o-whirl and were going to lose their lunch.

Slade asked, "Which way to the boardwalk?"

"Follow me. I know what area he's talking about."

They skirted Luna Park, and she pointed down some wooden steps that led to the sand. "Down there."

When they reached the bottom, there was a slab of cement tucked beneath the boardwalk and two rows of faded blue metal lockers gaping at them.

Slade put out a hand for a high five and she smacked his palm. "This is it, and there can't be too many possibilities, since it looks like only a few are in use."

Nicole swooped in on the first bank of lockers, her sneakers scuffing the sand beneath her feet. "And someone did most of the work for us already by leaving the doors ajar."

Walking down the first row, she called out when she saw a closed and locked locker. Slade followed her, trying the key on each.

She tapped a locker in the middle of the second row. "Here's another one."

Slade stepped in front of her, slipped the key in and turned the lock with a click. "Bingo."

Leaning her chin on his arm, she asked, "Is it in there?"

"Yep." Slade dragged out a padded oblong goldenrod envelope and ripped off the top. He puckered it open and peeked inside, then showed it to her. "It's a mini computer disc."

"Oh, my God. We found it." Nicole twirled on her toes on the sandy cement. "It's over."

"Just about." Slade folded over the top of the envelope and stuffed it in the inside pocket of his jacket. "Get on the phone and text Pierre and let's get out of here."

Nicole sent Pierre a text and then jogged up the wooden stairs with a lighter step than on the way down. They passed in front of the entrance to Luna Park, and she sniffed the air as a distinct deep-fried odor wafted on the breeze. "Pierre's corn dog."

She veered toward the entrance, digging in her pocket for her ticket stub. "I can't find my ticket, and we didn't get our hands stamped."

Slade held up his own ticket stub. "I'll get it. Wait here."

She leaned against the front gate, watching Slade as he strode to the same corn dog stand that was in Trudy's picture. What a stroke of luck it had been finding that picture.

The long black car pulled up to the curb where the buses usually parked, and she waved to Pierre. She couldn't see him through those tinted windows, but he could see her.

She glanced over her shoulder at Slade waiting in line and pointed toward the car, which he probably couldn't see. He'd figure it out when he left the park and saw the town car.

She walked to the waiting car and slid into the backseat. She tapped on the divider window to let Pierre know his corn dog was on the way.

The car lurched forward and squealed away from the curb. The violence of the motion threw Nicole back against the seat. Didn't he realize Slade wasn't in the car, and what was the big hurry, anyway?

She pounded on the glass with her fist and shouted, "Pierre, stop. We left Slade behind."

The partition glided open and someone pointed a gun at her through the space, and then a face followed.

"We left Slade behind? That's even better."

Chapter Fifteen

Where the hell was Nicole going? She usually followed orders without question. What had she been pointing at?

"Can you hurry it up a little?"

The pimply-faced kid pushed his paper cap back on his head. "You wanted three, right?"

"Just give me one." He jabbed his finger at the corn dog wrapped in foil on the tray next to the deep fryer.

The guy handed it to him, and Slade snatched it and swung away from the window.

"Sir, you already paid for three."

"Keep the change."

With his heart hammering, Slade jogged out of the park. Nicole was no longer standing by the gate. She was gone.

He forced himself to breathe. Maybe she'd walked to the designated meeting place with Pierre ahead of him. She should've waited. They weren't out of the woods yet.

With a quickening pace to match his quickening pulse, Slade turned the corner toward the main parking area and swallowed. No car. No Nicole.

He dropped the corn dog into a trash can and made a beeline for the meeting place. Where had Pierre gone? Could security have waved off the car and Pierre made a circle around the parking lot with Nicole in the backseat?

He peered over the sea of cars in the parking lot and caught his breath when he saw a black town car hauling ass through the exit. That couldn't be their car. That couldn't be Pierre. The driver had checked out. Slade wouldn't have allowed Nicole in the car with just any driver.

A scattering of people stared at him as they made their way toward the amusement parks. He must look as frantic as he felt.

As he stuffed his hand in his pocket to retrieve his phone, he heard a low moan. He froze. He cocked his head to one side and heard it again.

He stepped off the curb, following the sound around the back end of a bus. His gut lurched when he saw Pierre's bloodied and battered form leaning against the back tire of the bus.

Slade crouched beside the driver, whose face had been beaten and whose hands clutched at his midsection, where blood oozed through his fingers.

"My God, what happened?" Slade punched in 911 on his cell.

"Sorry. I got out of the car for a smoke. They snuck up on me, punched me a few times and knifed me in the gut." He coughed and gurgled, and a trickle of blood leaked from the corner of his mouth.

A woman behind Slade yelped. "Is he okay?"

"I'm on with 911 now." Slade gave instructions to the 911 operator as he pulled off his jacket and then ripped off his shirt. He nudged Pierre's hands away from his wound and pressed his shirt against it to try to stop the bleeding. "EMTs should be on the way soon. Hang in there, man."

"Nicole?"

"Gone. I think they got her." Slade pressed harder against Pierre's stomach with both hands. "I'm assuming they took the car."

Pierre gasped and nodded.

A few more people gathered behind Slade, tossing questions at him that he had no intention of answering unless one of them was a doctor.

A siren keened in the distance, and Slade cranked his head over his shoulder to the onlookers. "Make sure the emergency personnel know where to go. Wave them over here to the bus."

Several people murmured behind him, but they all sounded on board.

Pierre's eyelids fluttered. "Nicole."

"It's okay, Pierre. I'll find her." He *had* to find her.

"P-pocket."

Slade leaned close to Pierre's mouth. "What?"

"Right. Jacket. Pocket."

Slade jammed his hand into the pocket of Pierre's ripped black suit jacket, his fingers colliding with a hard, square object. He yanked it out. "What is it?"

The ambulance screeched to a halt behind him and the EMTs jumped out and rushed toward them, dispersing the crowd.

"What happened to him?"

Slade cleared his throat, curling his fingers around the object from Pierre's pocket. "Someone beat him up and knifed him. Bad wound in his stomach."

Pierre's eyes opened again, and he grabbed Slade's sleeve. "Right jacket pocket."

Again, Slade ducked his head as the EMTs tried to shove him to the side. "I have it, Pierre. What is it?"

Pierre's bloody lips stretched across his teeth in a macabre smile. "GPS for the car."

Slade fell back, allowing the EMTs to get to work on Pierre. He put his jacket back on over his bare torso, feeling for the mini disc in the inner pocket, and dragged himself to a bench around the corner. He didn't need to talk to the police right now.

Cupping the GPS in his bloodstained hands, he studied it.

Pierre, or the car service, must have it linked to a tracking device on the car. He turned it over in his hand and noticed the USB port. He needed to access a computer—fast. Who knew how long Nicole's abductors would stay in that car?

Where the hell could he get to a computer out here? He didn't have time to go all the way back to the Upper East Side.

He pulled out his phone and searched for the nearest library and got a hit a few miles away. Damn. He needed a car. His gaze shifted across the blanket of cars in the parking lot.

He didn't like the idea of ruining someone's day at Coney Island, but he didn't have a second to waste, and he couldn't hang around here anymore for the cops to question him about the attack on Pierre.

Hunching into his jacket, he ducked behind a car and weaved his way through the lot, keeping an eye out for a likely vehicle to hot-wire. Not only would he not be talking to the police, he'd be stealing a car beneath their noses. So much for his low profile.

Fifteen minutes later he was wheeling out of the parking lot in a late-model sedan and heading to the nearest library.

On the way, he tried Nicole's number, but as he expected, not even her voice mail picked up. Most likely her captors had disabled her phone so it couldn't be pinged.

When Slade reached the library, he parked the stolen car in plain sight—no sense in trying to hide it, but the police wouldn't be looking for a stolen car at the library, anyway. He parked himself in front of a public computer and connected the GPS.

The application for accessing the car's data was straightforward, and Slade's heart skipped a beat when he saw the car still moving in an eastward direction. Then it skipped another beat when he realized they could be heading to the airport.

He wasn't doing any good following the car's—and Nicole's—progress on a computer screen. He had to get this GPS tracking data on his phone so he could follow them in his new car.

He entered an SOS communication on his phone to the number for tech support he'd been given earlier. After several back-and-forth messages and entries on the computer and his phone, the folks in tech were able to download the GPS data he needed.

He sent another terse missive to Ariel to let her know he had the film but was on his way to rescue Nicole. If Ariel believed his mission was over now that he had Lars's footage in his hands, she didn't know the Navy SEAL sniper team.

The computer cranked and whirred as he cleared all his history from it, or at least as much as he knew how. Tapping his phone, he activated the GPS as he exited the library and hopped into the car. He'd left out the part about the stolen vehicle in his email to Ariel, but he'd make sure somehow it was returned to that Coney Island parking lot and its rightful owners.

Starting off with a lead foot as he followed the

magic yellow dot on his display, he soon eased up. The last thing he needed was to get pulled over and arrested for stealing a car. Nicole needed him, and he was going to deliver.

The car moved closer and closer to JFK, and with every inch, Slade's stomach dipped. They couldn't very well haul a kicking and screaming woman onto a commercial flight—and he had no doubt Nicole would be kicking and screaming—but what if they had a private plane stashed at the airport? What if they planned to take Nicole away? What if they'd already knocked her out? Sedated her? Killed her?

He slammed his hands against the steering wheel. *No!* They needed her to get the film from him. They must know by now she didn't have the disc on her. They'd use her to get the film from him—*then* they'd kill her…and him, too.

Suddenly, the yellow dot on the display stopped moving in an area near the airport—validating Slade's darkest fear. He continued heading in the direction of the town car, the stationary yellow indicator acting like a beacon of hope for him. Even though it had stopped moving, it was all he had—all he had left of Nicole.

Slade drove for another forty-five minutes, panic rising in his gut as he kept one eye on the unmoving target. The GPS led him to a parking structure about a half mile out from the airport, and he glided down the second level until he spotted the black town car with the tinted windows.

He didn't expect them to be sitting there waiting for him, but he drew his weapon anyway and approached the car silently from the side, gun at the ready.

Releasing a long breath, he tried the door while peering in the window. At least they'd had the courtesy to lock up.

He broke the window with the butt of his gun and quickly disabled the alarm system. He brushed the glass from the driver's seat before sliding in and shutting the door behind him.

Placing his hands on the steering wheel, he inhaled Nicole's lingering scent in the car. Then he shook his head. Daydreaming about Nicole was not going to save her.

He started searching the car—the seats, the floor, the glove compartment. Then he tried his luck in the backseat. Nicole's scent was even stronger here, and in a strange way it gave him hope. Bending forward, he inspected the floor and saw the corner of a white piece of paper peeking out from the floor mat.

He freed it and shook out a dirty envelope, but it was so much more than that. Nicole had jotted down a few quick notes. She'd been able to tell him about the two men who'd abducted her—Conrad, Trudy's ex, and a stranger with a French accent.

French? The gunman in the club who'd killed Dahir was French.

So, Nicole had left a few clues. How had she known he'd find the car? Had she known about the GPS or did she just have some ridiculously misplaced faith in his superpowers because he'd saved her once before?

That rescue operation had been child's play compared to this. He was no spook, but he'd have to pretend to be one. Just as he was working out a plan to try to track their movements, his cell phone rang.

He glanced at his cell, which showed Nicole's number on the display. He didn't have to track them after all. They'd reached out to him.

He answered. "Yeah?"

Conrad's voice, his German accent more pronounced, greeted him. "Hello, *Steve*, although we all know you're really Slade Gallagher. Do you have the disc?"

"Do you have Nicole?"

"You know we do."

"Safe? I want to speak with her."

"Fair enough, but just know my associate has a gun pointed at her head in case she tries something funny."

Hot anger pounded behind Slade's eyes, and he squeezed them closed for a second. "Put her on."

Nicole's voice, sounding firmer than Conrad's, came on the line. "I'm sorry, Slade. I should've waited for you at the gate. I got into the car, and this scumbag pulled a gun on me. At least you have the film footage. Take it wherever it can be analyzed and don't worry..."

She grunted and Slade gripped his phone so hard it cut into the sides of his hand. "Don't touch her."

"She tried funny business. You're not going to listen to her, are you, Navy SEAL hero? You bring us the disc and we'll hand her over to you."

Yeah, right.

"Where are you?"

"I suppose we don't have to tell you that if you bring anyone with you, she's dead on the spot. No questions. We hear a siren, a helicopter, a boat, see anyone other than you approaching...*ffft.*"

The noise Gunther made sounded like a silencer, whether he meant it or not, but Slade got the idea. Slade wasn't sure he'd trust the chain of command to rescue Nicole, anyway. They'd want the disc first and foremost.

"I'll come alone. Where are you?"

"Where are *you*? Still at Coney Island?"

Slade's mind whirred into action. "No. I'm back in Manhattan."

"Then it should take you a while to get here."

That's what Slade was hoping he'd think. Conrad had no reason to believe otherwise.

"Where's here? Where do you want me to go?"

Conrad whispered something Slade couldn't catch

and then spoke up. "We're in a little seaside town about halfway between the airport and Montauk. Since it's going to take you a long time to get out here, let's set up this little meeting for later tonight. We have a few things to arrange first, anyway."

So did he.

"Give me the time and the location."

Conrad reeled off the directions, and Slade scribbled them down on the envelope Nicole had used to describe her captors.

"We'll have Nicole on the beach in front of the house at ten o'clock. We'll be able to see your arrival from land, air or sea, and if you do anything other than approach us with your hands up, Nicole is dead. If you try to show up before the appointed time, Nicole is dead. If we see any suspicious activity on the beach in the hours before our meeting time, Nicole is dead. Got it?"

"Got it." Slade ended the call and immediately placed another.

He'd bring Conrad the disc, all right, but he had no intention of giving it to him in some phony exchange for Nicole.

He'd see him dead first.

Chapter Sixteen

Nicole shifted on the uncomfortable chair, her arms tied behind her back. She'd tried to escape once after they'd given her some food and had gotten a kick to the small of her back for her efforts.

She didn't want Slade to give up that disc. Too many people had died trying to protect it. If she had to be the next in line, so be it.

Her gaze darted between the two of them, speaking German, their faces devoid of emotion, and she swallowed hard. Yes, they would really kill her.

She surveyed the front room of the small seaside cottage that had to be worth a couple of mil. They must've rented it…or maybe they'd just broken in.

How would they have known about the trip to Coney Island? They probably followed them or somehow gotten their travel information from the car company. Maybe they'd scouted out this location earlier or just figured it was a deserted enough spot to carry out the exchange.

Slade would have to be a fool to think these two men would simply allow him to give them the disc and saunter off with her into the sunset—and Slade was no fool.

Knitting her eyebrows, she glanced out the window at the Frenchman strolling in front of the house, back and forth, back and forth. He wasn't taking any chances of a surprise attack.

What could Slade do at this point? If he came in shooting, Conrad and his buddy would kill her. And with Frenchie out there on patrol, Slade, and whoever he might bring with him, had no opportunity to take them by surprise.

There were boats docked at a small pier several yards down the beach, but there was no way Slade could come in on a boat without being noticed.

She chewed on her bottom lip. She'd heard the meeting time was ten o'clock, and it had to be close to that now—and she was still sitting here.

She eyed Conrad and cleared her throat. "How did you kill Trudy?"

Conrad looked up from his phone and glanced over his shoulder at Frenchie making one of his endless rounds. She'd already figured out pretty quickly that the Frenchman discouraged any communication with her, and the majority of his exchanges with Conrad were in German, which she didn't understand. He wanted to keep her in the dark.

But Conrad liked to talk. He liked to brag, and if

she was going down tonight, she at least wanted to know what it was all for.

He shrugged. "Trudy had epilepsy."

"Which you used somehow to cause her death and make it look like her condition was at fault."

"It wasn't hard, really. I replaced her medication with…something else. I was going for the dramatic. I thought she'd collapse in the middle of the play, which needed something to liven it up." He rolled his eyes. "You saw it. Dreadful."

Nicole gritted her teeth. "And the woman walking my dog?"

"Sloppy, I agree. I'm actually glad that turned out the way it did, since she wasn't you anyway, and I do like dogs."

"It's just the two of you? Where are the rest of your buddies?" She strained against the rope binding her wrists. There had to be a way she could help Slade so that they both didn't die.

"Buddies?"

"There's you, the sniper in the park outside the bar and the man who followed us on the train—Marcus Friedrich—the one who rigged that house in Queens with the explosives." She tossed her head back to get the hair out of her face. "Marcus was ID'd from the prints on his gun. Not too bright, is he?"

"That's why he excused himself from this operation."

"So, that man—" she tipped her chin at the window "—is the sniper from the park?"

Conrad narrowed his eyes as if trying to figure out where her line of questioning was leading. He pressed his lips together, probably figuring his French friend was right—better to keep mum about the details of their operation.

"The shooter in The Blues Joint was French, too, but he's dead. How'd you get Dahir to cooperate with you and lure me out? His family?"

"Dahir Musse's family is gone."

Nicole blinked, feeling the blood drain from her face.

Conrad grinned and then studied his fingernails. "My turn. What's your SEAL doing operating in the States? Isn't that illegal or something? Maybe I should report him."

He seemed to think this was hilarious, since he giggled for several seconds.

She dragged in a deep breath to clear the shock of the news about Dahir's family.

Conrad could be lying about that, and he wasn't too bright, either, since he'd just revealed it was just the two of them and Slade wouldn't have to deal with a third party. Not that it did a whole lot of good, since the two here had a clear view of all approaches to the cottage and a gun to her head whenever they needed it, and of course, Slade didn't know how many he'd have to handle.

And he *could* handle them—she had faith in the rich boy.

A knock on the front door had her jumping out

of her skin, and then the Frenchman called out, "It's time. Bring her out. No chances. Do you understand?"

Conrad snorted lightly. "*Oui, ja*, yes."

He picked up his gun from the table and pointed it at her. "Get up very slowly. I don't have to tell you. At this point, any move you make out of the ordinary will result in your death. Do you understand?"

"*Oui, ja*, yes."

Smirking, he waved at her with the barrel of his gun.

Licking her lips, she rose to her feet, her gaze pinned to the window and the darkness beyond. Slade was out there somewhere, and she hoped he had a hell of a plan.

SLADE SURFACED AND hauled his weapons bag onto the boat, keeping out of view of the beach just about a half a mile away. As he peeled off his wet suit, his friend and team member Josh Elliot broke the surface of the water and joined him.

"You for sure know there are just two of them?" Josh unzipped his own weapons bag and yanked out his .300 Win Mag.

Cradling the M107, his weapon of choice, Slade said, "Two grabbed her. They might've picked up more along the way or met someone at that house, but I don't know. I guess we'll find out soon enough."

Josh slid his scope in place. "Isn't this exactly how

you met this woman? She's the one who was on that boat when we took down those four pirates, right?"

"I wouldn't say we exactly met at that time—only through my finder."

"It's a helluva way to pick up women, bro."

They worked in silence, breathing heavily as they assembled their sniper rifles—or maybe that was just *his* breathing. He'd never been more nervous before an operation.

He'd never been in love with a rescue subject before, either.

As soon as he'd learned how much time he'd have to prepare, he knew what he had to do to rescue Nicole. That spy stuff wasn't his strong suit, but this? *Second nature, baby.*

He'd made a few calls, arranged to have some weapons delivered and managed to locate one of his team members, Josh Elliot, who happened to be in the States preparing for a trip to South America for some reason he wouldn't reveal to Slade.

Studying a map of the area and the coastline revealed exactly what he needed to do to get close to the house without being seen. The terrorists' first mistake was doing the exchange on the beach.

He got it. They'd figured the beach would be deserted at night, a reasonable place to hold a woman at gunpoint. They'd also reasoned that on the beach, in the open, Slade wouldn't be able to sneak up on them, bringing other people with him.

Guess they forgot about the *sea* part in SEAL, because they had to know who he was by now.

Josh grunted as he positioned his weapon. "The powers that be think it's Vlad we're dealing with, don't they?"

"I may have heard his name once or twice."

"You know what that means, don't you? He's luring each one of us out, one by one. You know about Foley's run-in with Vlad's operatives in Boston, don't you?"

"Yep." He slid a sideways glance at Josh. "Are you up next?"

Josh rolled his shoulders. "Bring it on."

Slade grinned at his good luck in finding Josh stateside. Josh was one tough SOB, all about justice—his own brand.

Josh clicked his tongue. "Looky, looky. They're waiting for you."

Slade shifted forward, aiming his weapon at the beach—two men, just as Nicole had indicated—and Nicole. This was how he remembered first seeing her—strong, fearless, standing tall with a gun at her head.

"I'll take the guy who has Nicole. You can have the other guy."

"Of course you'll take the guy who has Nicole— *hero.*"

And just like last time, Nicole shifted away from her captor. Could she sense his presence? "You ready,

Josh? They're going to start getting antsy in about one minute."

"No time like the present, dude."

Slade tightened his finger on the trigger and did the honors. "Five, four, three, two..."

The terrorists on the beach dropped. Never knew what hit 'em.

This time Nicole didn't spit on the body at her feet. She turned her face to the ocean and raised two thumbs.

Chapter Seventeen

Hours later, with the light of day making its first appearance, Nicole hovered over the back of the sofa where Slade sat, hunched over his laptop.

"Here we go." Slade tapped the keyboard. "I don't think I've ever anticipated a movie more than this one."

"Does Ariel know you're having a peek at the footage before sending it off?"

"Yeah, she wants me to—and I'm going to send it off to them right now, anyway. They can have a copy while we look at this one." He took her hand and kissed the inside of her wrist. "Conrad and Frenchie are gone and Marcus Friedrich may be on the run, but there are others to take their place. The sooner we figure out the significance of this film, the better."

She came around from the back of the sofa and sat beside him, her shoulder meeting his.

Slade double clicked the video file, and as the

film came to life on the monitor, Nicole covered her mouth with one hand.

"Look, it's all of us." She jabbed her finger at the image on the screen. "Me, Giles and Dahir."

She was giving instructions to Lars, who was laughing and cutting up, while Giles was making goofy faces. Now they were all gone, including Dahir's family. A sob bubbled in her throat, and Slade put his arm around her, pulling her even closer.

The footage switched from the four of them joking around to Lars testing his focus on her practicing interview questions to Giles and Dahir in a deep discussion. Then the interviews started.

Tears blurred her vision as she watched the brave interview subjects talk about their lives and their hopes and dreams and the courageous acts they were taking to make those hopes and dreams come true. She sniffed. "I hope one day I can tell their stories."

"This is incredible stuff." Slade squeezed the back of her neck. "You did some amazing work here."

They continued to watch the film. Lars had already done quite a bit of work on it, merging all the different shoots into one. The story, with Nicole's narration, took them from village to village, from town to town, including shots of the war-torn countryside and their trips in the ramshackle Jeep with Giles at the wheel and Dahir getting them out of some tight spots. Too bad he hadn't been able to get himself out of the tightest spot.

"I don't see it." Slade ran a hand through his short sandy-blond hair. "Unless this well-oiled terrorist organization, which was responsible for two deaths overseas and two more here, wanted to stop these women from speaking out, I just don't understand their frantic need to stop this footage from going live."

"There was that woman's husband who walked in on us. Go back to that."

"Where was it?"

"I scribbled it down on this sticky note." She plucked a pink note from the edge of the laptop screen and read the time aloud. "It's at forty-three, thirty-two, fifty-one."

Slade's hand froze above the keyboard. "What did you say?"

She waved the note stuck to her finger. "Forty-three, thirty-two, fifty-one."

He snapped his fingers. "The note. Dahir's note in the club. Where is it?"

"By the telephone. Do you want it?"

"Please."

She crossed the room to the kitchen and grabbed the note, still smudged with Dahir's blood. When she glanced at the numbers, she squealed. "It's a time stamp of the footage."

"Exactly. Read off those numbers."

As she bolted back to the sofa, she recited, "Fifteen, twenty-three, nineteen."

She parked herself next to Slade again as he dragged the indicator back to the fifteen-minute mark.

Pointing at the screen, she said, "This is where we talked to that woman outside in that noisy area near the town of Badhadhe."

"Can you switch up the focus, away from her and more to the background?"

"Of course, but we have to go outside of the film Lars created and to the individual footage. Pause this and get to the other files."

Slade followed her instructions and soon they were looking at the raw footage of that interview.

Hunching in closer, Slade said, "Watch that road in the background. There's a truck going through that gate. Another truck. Look at the men at the entrance."

Her gaze shifted to two men talking across the road from the interview. One looked directly into the camera and pointed. The other turned around.

Slade froze the frame and jabbed his finger at one of the men. "Nicole, he's a known terrorist. That gate and the road across the street from this woman's home leads to a terrorist training camp. *That's* what they didn't want us to see. *That's* why they ordered pirates to kidnap you and your crew—to kill you and destroy your film. But the pirates had their own ideas, and the film got away from the terrorist group running that camp—and now it's in our hands."

She broke down then, covered her face with both hands and cried like a baby.

LATER THAT MORNING, Slade got the word that a drone strike had lain waste to the terrorist training ground on the outskirts of Badhadhe.

When he got the news, Nicole poured two glasses of wine and brought one to Slade, standing at the window and gazing into the street below. "The homes near that training camp weren't hit, were they? Those people we talked to…?"

"Spared. The training camp was far inside that initial entry gate." He clinked his glass with hers and said, "Vlad got the message loud and clear."

"The CIA is sure this Vlad guy is behind the training camp and the effort to find the footage?" *And all the other death and destruction that followed.*

"I received a report from Ariel, along with the news of the drone strike. All of the operatives— Conrad, whose real name was William Brandt, the French sniper, the other Frenchman and Marcus Friedrich—can all be linked to Vlad."

"But you don't know Vlad's real name or even his nationality, do you?"

"No, but he's coming in hard. His terrorist cells are international, and we don't know his endgame… yet. My team has sparred with Vlad before. We just nicknamed him Vlad because he favors a Russian sniper rifle."

"You've sparred with him before, and he seems to know all of you."

"He knows we were the ones who rescued your crew from the pirates."

"And then he tried to take each one of us down. Do you believe that was all about the film or all about you?"

Slade swirled the wine in his glass. "Oh, he wanted that film, all right. Look what happened when we got our hands on it. But the fact that it was our rescue? He's taking a certain pleasure in that."

Nicole shivered and took a gulp of wine. Hopefully this was over for Slade, but what about his teammates?

She nudged his arm as he took a sip of his wine. "Too bad your friend Josh had to leave so quickly. He was pretty hot in that intense, mean-streets kinda way—obviously not a rich California boy."

"Definitely not." He tugged on a strand of her hair. "I thought you were giving up on the adventurous sort."

She gazed at him over the rim of her wineglass. "Never."

The look in his blue eyes made her heart skip several beats, but she had other news to share. "Oh, I called the hospital where Pierre is staying. He's out of the woods. He's going to be okay."

"Thank God. And Livvy?"

"Healing nicely and enjoying Chanel's company."

"Good, because she's going to have Chanel's company for a while when you join your mother in Italy."

She set her wineglass down on the windowsill and grabbed the front of Slade's shirt. "I thought you detested frivolous society girls with front-row seats at the fashion shows."

He placed his glass next to hers and rested his hands on her hips. "When that society girl is also a kick-ass filmmaker who can change the world, I can excuse a little haute couture."

He kissed her long and hard just to make his point. "And what about you? I thought you were ready to settle down with an accountant whose only risk was drinking a chardonnay with a steak."

"When that risk taker also happens to be saving the world, one life, one bullet at a time, I can grit my teeth and bear it." She smoothed her hands over his face. "As long as he comes back to me."

"Where else would I go? I love you, Nicole Hastings. You're in my blood and have been ever since I saw you on that pirate boat in the Gulf of Aden."

"I love you, too, rich boy."

"Does that mean you'll wait for me? I have at least one more tour, maybe two."

"What else would a snooty society girl have to do?" She tugged on the hem of his T-shirt. "Now, follow me. We have two days together before you have to go back to saving the world."

He swept her up in his arms effortlessly and nuzzled her neck as he carried her up the stairs. "The world can wait."

* * * * *

Look for more books in Carol Ericson's gripping miniseries
RED, WHITE AND BUILT
later in 2017.

You'll find them wherever Harlequin Intrigue books are sold!

SPECIAL EXCERPT FROM

H HARLEQUIN®

INTRIGUE

*Detective Ronan Cavanaugh O'Bannon will do
whatever it takes to protect one of the Cavanaughs' own
from a serial killer sweeping through Aurora, including
working with wild-card detective Sierra Carlyle.*

*Read on for a sneak preview of
CAVANAUGH STANDOFF,
the next book in USA TODAY bestselling author
Marie Ferrarella's fan-favorite series
CAVANAUGH JUSTICE.*

He knew he had to utilize her somehow, and maybe
she could be useful. "All right, you might as well come
along. You might come in handy if there's a next of kin
to notify." Ronan began walking back to his car. "I'm not
much good at that."

"I'm surprised," Sierra commented.

Reaching the car, Ronan turned to look at her. "If
you're going to be sarcastic—"

"No, I'm serious," she told him, then went on to
explain her rationale. "You're so detached, I just assumed
it wouldn't bother you to tell a person that someone
they'd expected to come home was never going to do that
again. It would bother them, of course," she couldn't help
adding, "but not you."

Ronan got into his vehicle, buckled up and pulled
out in what seemed like one fluid motion, all the while

chewing on what this latest addition to his team had just said. Part of him just wanted to let it go. But he couldn't.

"I'm not heartless," he informed her. "I just don't allow emotions to get in the way and I don't believe in using more words than are absolutely necessary," he added pointedly since he knew that seemed to bother her.

"Well, lucky for you, I do," she told him with what amounted to the beginnings of a smile. "I guess that's what'll make us such good partners."

He looked at her, stunned. He viewed them as being like oil and water—never able to mix. "Is that your take on this?" he asked incredulously.

"Yes," she answered cheerfully.

The fact that she appeared to have what one of his brothers would label a "killer smile" notwithstanding, Ronan just shook his head. "Unbelievable."

"Oh, you'll get to believe it soon enough," she told him. Before he could say anything, Sierra just continued talking to him and got down to the immediate business at hand. "I'm going to need to see your files on the other murders once we're back in the squad room so I can be brought up to date."

He didn't even spare her a look. "Fine."

"Are you always this cheerful?" she asked. "Or is there something in particular that's bothering you?"

Don't miss
CAVANAUGH STANDOFF by Marie Ferrarella,
available June 2017 wherever
Harlequin® Intrigue books and ebooks are sold.

www.Harlequin.com

THE WORLD IS BETTER WITH

Romance

Harlequin has everything from contemporary, passionate and heartwarming to suspenseful and inspirational stories.

Whatever your mood, we have a romance just for you!

Connect with us to find your next great read, special offers and more.

f /HarlequinBooks

@HarlequinBooks

www.HarlequinBlog.com

www.Harlequin.com/Newsletters

HARLEQUIN®

A *Romance* FOR EVERY MOOD™

www.Harlequin.com